ALSO BY JO DAVIS

FACE THE FLAMES

A SUGARLAND BLUE NOVEL

JO DAVIS

BERKLEY SENSATION
New York

BERKLEY SENSATION
Published by Berkley
An imprint of Penguin Random House LLC
375 Hudson Street, New York, New York 10014

ISBN: 9780451477002

First Edition: March 2017

Printed in the United States of America
1   3   5   7   9   10   8   6   4   2

To you. My readers who've been with me, loving my boys in Sugarland since the beginning. It's been a helluva ride, hasn't it? But wait—maybe I'm not quite ready to say good-bye to my Sugarland heroes just yet.

Just maybe, there are one or two stories still waiting to be told.

For now, Clay's story is for you. With love.

Acknowledgments

With special thanks to:

My beautiful daughter and handsome son, who are my champions and the light of my life. I love you both so very much.

My parents, who support me unfailingly and hold me up when I fall. I love you both to the moon and back.

To my dearest friends for making me laugh when I want to cry, and for forcing me into the world when I'd rather hide. You know who you are, and I love you all.

To my agent, Nephele Tempest, for encouraging me and believing in me.

To all the great people at Penguin/Berkley for working so hard to put out my books and make me the best I can be.

From the bottom of my heart.

Prologue

"Got a hot date tomorrow night, right?"

Clay Montana stepped out of the shower, grabbed a towel off the hook on the wall next to the stall, and rubbed his head vigorously. God, it felt great to get the stink of the grass fire out of his hair and off his skin. That shit *lingered*.

Toweling off his torso, he shot his friend a grin. Julian Salvatore was a fellow firefighter/paramedic at Fire Station Five. "Why? You want a piece of this fine, Grade-A beef? You'll have to stand in line, buddy."

Julian barked a laugh and jerked on a fresh pair of uniform pants. "Um, no. Grace has me covered in that department, trust me."

"Your loss, Sylvie's gain." He thought a second. "Or is it Tracy?"

"You hound dog." Julian shook his head.

"And you're a poor, old *reformed* hound dog. I'll bet you have to ask permission to have a beer with the guys, and even have a joint Facebook account with the sweetie. How sad is that?" Clay shot his friend a look of sympathy and got the finger in return.

"I don't even *have* a Facebook account."

"Not helping your case."

"Whatever," Julian grumbled, pulling on his shirt. "At least I know I'm going home to a beautiful woman who loves me, every single night. You should try it sometime. You know, someone who loves you, besides your *madre*."

Why that barb stung so much, Clay wasn't sure. He wasn't ready to settle down. Right? He was enjoying the hell out of his wild and free bachelorhood, so why not live it up while he was still young? And who cared if the only woman in his life was his mother?

"My mother is a goddess, just so you know," he said in Charlene's defense as he pulled on his clothes.

"So's mine, but a man needs more in the way of a positive female relationship, eventually." Julian paused and his dark eyes widened. "Shit, listen to me. Maybe I have gotten a little domesticated."

"More like totally pussy-whipped."

Laughing, Clay dodged the playful punch to his shoulder. As Julian walked out of the men's common shower area, Clay caught a glimpse of himself in the mirror and paused. His smile died as he stared at himself, a kernel of truth in what his friend had said bothering him a little.

What did his playmates think when they looked at him? He wasn't really a vain man, but he knew he was good-looking and didn't mind employing the tools nature gave him when it came to having a good time. At just over six feet, with messy sandy blond hair, blue eyes, and a lean, muscled build, he cut a decent enough figure.

But Julian's words made him wonder whether anyone special would ever bother to look beneath the surface and really *see* him.

"Is there anything worth seeing?" he muttered. Then he snorted at his sudden, uncharacteristic moment of self-reflection, pushed the idea aside, and left the showers.

As he strode into the kitchen, the station's lieutenant, Zack Knight, was arguing with their captain, Howard "Six-Pack" Paxton, over who was going to get the last of the chocolate chip cookies Clay had baked earlier.

"You ate a dozen already!" Zack protested, trying to reach the cookie Six-Pack was holding way out of reach. "Give me that, you big thug!"

Six-Pack grinned at the shorter, slimmer man.

"Possession is nine-tenths of the law. If you can take it from me, you can have it, squirt."

Nearby, Eve Tanner chortled and Clay joined in. Jamie Blackburn, the newest guy on the team, just watched from his spot on the sofa. Zack, at just over six feet tall himself, was definitely no squirt. It was just that Howard was so fucking *huge* at six feet six inches and around two-fifty or so, that nobody dared to fuck with him. Except, apparently, when it came to the last chocolate chip cookie.

Around here, that was serious shit.

"Uh, guys, I can make another batch," Clay offered. "They came from a box of mix, so it wasn't exactly rocket science."

Zack stopped reaching and turned to Clay, his gaze hopeful. "You'll make more?"

"I just said I would."

"Good thing, too," Six-Pack said, popping the whole cookie into his mouth and chewing in bliss. "Mmm."

Zack scowled at the big captain. "You're such a jerk sometimes."

"But you love me."

"No. I really, really don't."

The lieutenant seemed somewhat mollified, however, as Clay moved into the kitchen and retrieved another box of cookie mix from the pantry. Unfortunately, before Clay could even reach to turn on the oven, three loud tones over the intercom system alerted them to an incoming call. A collective groan filled the kitchen—after the grass fire, nobody was looking forward to another callout so soon. Especially to a major traffic accident.

Abandoning the cookies for the time being, Clay followed his captain and lieutenant out of the side door leading into the bay. As he did, his gaze snagged on the words etched into the glass of the door:

Everybody Goes Home.

The first time he'd ever read them, on his very first shift as a firefighter, they'd caused a shiver down his spine. On every shift since then, they'd never failed to do the same. So many of their friends over the years hadn't made it home. Clay couldn't help but wonder when or if his number would be up one day.

His morbid thoughts were interrupted as Julian called, "You drive."

Clay barely reacted in time to catch the keys to the ambulance. "I drove last time, man. It's your turn."

"Consider it a favor."

"You feeling okay?"

"Yeah. Just don't feel like driving."

"Maybe I don't, either." They didn't have time to argue about it, though. And what did it matter anyway? Clay shrugged and walked around to the driver's side. "Sure. But you owe me."

"Thanks."

Pulling out of the bay, Clay hit the lights and the siren. Behind him, Zack followed in the big quint carrying Six-Pack, Jamie, and Eve. Julian manned the

GPS, giving him directions to their call, and then they settled back for the ride.

After a few moments, Julian's thoughtful voice broke the silence. "So, what do you think about Jamie?"

"Honestly, I'm not sure yet. He seems a little quiet, but I don't know if that's because the rest of us are so rowdy or because he really doesn't have much to say."

"Or just doesn't want to fit in."

"Could be." Clay thought for a moment. "I don't really think that's it, though. My guess is he's got a story and he's not ready to open up to the group."

"You're probably right. He's a nice guy, just . . . reserved."

"He never hesitates on a call to jump in and do what needs to be done," Clay said thoughtfully. "The rest, we can work on."

Julian made a sound of agreement and they fell silent for a few moments as Clay navigated through the traffic near downtown. The flow wasn't too heavy today, but he was watchful as he threaded through the other vehicles, laying on the horn when necessary to alert traffic ahead to pull over and let them pass.

"*Dios*, people are idiots," Julian muttered as one guy in a Porsche hung in front of them, in the way, then moved over at the last second.

"Or they've got their music playing so loud, they can't hear us coming."

That was one of the most common dangers firefighters faced on calls every day that the public didn't much think about—drivers being so distracted by their radios or cell phones, arguments, or conversations with other passengers, that they caused accidents.

As they neared the site of the call, Clay's brain kicked into rescue mode. How bad was the wreck? What would they find when they got there?

At an intersection, the light turned green and he started through it.

What would—

"Clay!"

Julian's shout was all the warning he got. Turning his head to the left to look out his driver's window, he saw the front end of a truck barreling toward him. A shock of horror jolted through him as he realized there was no way to avoid the collision.

The grill rushed toward him and then—

Impact.

Blackness.

1

One year later

The sunny day, with just a hint of coolness in the air, was a fine one for a walk.

There were long months in recovery when Clay Montana didn't know whether he'd ever stand on his own two feet again, let alone take a stroll through the streets. Using his cane to help keep his balance, shuffling carefully along the sidewalk, he felt like an old man. He'd turned thirty years old in the Intensive Care Unit at Sterling, lying in a coma and unaware of the sad visitors and birthday balloons.

He'd come a long way since then, but thinking about how far he still had to go was daunting. In the beginning, he had wished he'd been killed outright—and he'd said so when he regained the ability to speak, in front of his mother, who started to cry. Charlene Montana was the strongest woman he'd ever known. She simply didn't cry.

Clay had never said something so stupid again. Not in front of his mom anyway.

When he was relearning how to walk, talk, feed, and dress himself, even go to the fucking bathroom . . . Yeah, he'd been tempted to give up, more than once. But too many people had worked hard to make sure he could step back into his life whenever he was ready, so he couldn't simply throw it all away.

His mother was a godsend. When she wasn't by his side praying for his survival, she was managing his finances, taking his checks, and paying his bills in his absence to make sure he didn't lose his house and car. His friends had pitched in as well, mowing his yard and doing endless chores to keep Clay's property in shape so he had one less worry when he was finally released from the hospital.

For a very long time, nobody had been certain he'd be leaving there alive.

The complications and setbacks had been many, some dangerous. But leave he had, and he'd lived with his mother at her house for months, until he'd finally argued that he was well enough to return to his own home—and had won.

Loneliness was his enemy now. He hated it, and had far too much time on his hands to think about how the world had gone on without him. Sure, he had his friends from the station, but they were busy with their own lives. Everyone on his team was paired off except for Jamie and himself, and they didn't have time to hold his hand anymore.

I want what they have. Someone to come home to. Somebody to love.

When had that happened? Did it even matter? Placing one foot in front of the other, he gave a grim chuckle at just how unlikely a love connection seemed for him these days. Every single one of his girlfriends had vanished like smoke when the going got tough.

The lesson was painful. He got out of those so-called relationships exactly what he'd put into them—not a damned thing.

Just then, his cell phone rang. Stumbling to a halt, he fished for the device and checked the caller ID. *Mom.* He let out a weary sigh. Wouldn't do him any good to ignore her. She'd keep calling until he answered. "Hey, Big Mama, how's it shakin'?"

No stuttering or hesitation in his speech today. That was real progress.

"If you don't stop calling me that," she huffed.

"You'll what? Knock me senseless? Been there."

"Clayton Lee!"

He winced. "Too soon, huh?"

"That'll *never* be funny." She sighed. "How are you feeling today, baby?"

The endearment warmed something inside him. Some guys might be embarrassed to be called that, but it reminded him that there was at least one person on the planet who loved him unconditionally and always would. His throat tightened.

"Pretty good. Didn't want to waste this nice day, so I'm out walking."

"Not overdoing it?"

"No, ma'am."

"When's your next checkup?"

Doctors, doctors, and more fucking doctors. He struggled not to let his irritation come through in his voice. "Day after tomorrow. I'm working on getting the clearance to get back to the station."

Silence. Coming from Charlene, it conveyed more than any amount of yelling ever could.

Then, "Oh, honey."

"I can do my job, Mom." His fingers clenched the phone, and he coached himself not to snap at his mother.

"Eventually. I just don't want you to push yourself too soon, and then be disappointed with the results."

"You mean when they tell me that my career is over."

"No, that's not what I meant at all. But if you try to go back before you're one hundred percent, it'll set back your recovery," she said, worried.

As if I don't know that.

He took a deep breath. "I'll be careful. Besides, do

you think I'd risk anyone's safety if I couldn't do the job? Or that my team would let me?"

"No, I just worry. I can't help it."

Guilt curled through his gut. His mom had been through so much, and for the past year his ordeal had consumed her life as well. "I know you do. I'm sorry."

"Nothing to be sorry about," she assured him softly. "I know how frustrated you are."

She did. The woman was a damned saint.

"So, dinner on Sunday?" he asked, changing the subject.

"As always, unless you have something else planned."

He laughed outright at that notion. "I'll check my busy social calendar and get back to you."

"Smartass." She snorted. "See you around five. Bring a friend if you want."

"Thanks, Mom. Love you."

"Love you, too, baby."

After he hung up, he contemplated her offer to bring a friend. She said it almost every time, but he had no idea who he'd invite. Maybe he'd just invite the whole gang over one Sunday, whoever could come. But he'd give her a little notice before he asked that many over.

As he continued on his way, he warmed to the idea. His mom would soak up the attention from his buddies like a sponge, and it would give her a crew to fuss over. The guys had become particularly fond of Charlene during Clay's ordeal, and the feeling was mutual. He was surprised he hadn't thought of inviting them all before.

Traffic began to get heavier, and with a start Clay realized he'd walked almost all the way downtown. Christ, he wasn't going to be able to make it back home on his own steam. He might have to call—

Pop, pop, pop.

Clay's steps faltered, and his head snapped up as he scanned the area for the source of the noise. Close by, but muffled, as though it had come from inside one of the buildings. *Please, don't let it be what it sounded like.*

Just then, a man slammed out the door of the gas station just ahead on the corner and took off on foot. The gun in the guy's hand shone briefly in the sun before he disappeared from view.

"Shit!"

Hurrying forward, Clay moved as fast as he could toward the gas station. There was no way he could pursue the gunman in his condition, and the potential victims inside were his top priority anyway. In moments, he was inside the station, checking the aisles. There didn't appear to be any customers.

"Hello?"

A groan answered, coming from behind the cash register. Limping in that direction, Clay reached the counter and looked around the end of it. A young clerk was sprawled on the floor, bleeding from his shoulder. He had a bloody hand over the wound, and his face was white. Damn, he couldn't be more than nineteen or so.

Propping his cane against the counter, Clay hurried to the boy's side and knelt, ignoring the flare of pain in his hip and knee. "You're gonna be all right, kid," he said in his most soothing tone.

And in that instant, a missing piece of himself snapped firmly back into place. The proper procedure was all there, waiting to be unlocked in his brain. It had only needed a trigger.

Too bad this poor kid was a victim of such horrible violence.

"That bastard shot me," the young man whispered, eyes wide. "I gave him the money, but he shot me anyway."

"Did you get a chance to hit the silent alarm?"

"Yeah."

"Good for you. Breathe, okay? You're going to be all right." Glancing around, he spotted a towel on a nearby shelf. After grabbing it, he returned to the boy's side.

"I want my dad," he said, eyes welling with tears.

"What's your name? I'm Clay, and I'm a paramedic." He applied pressure to the wound with one hand, checked his pulse with the other. Too fast.

"Drew Cooper."

Why the hell did that name sound so familiar?

"Who's your dad? We'll call him," he reassured Drew.

"Shane Ford," he rasped. "He's a detective here in town."

Clay froze for a moment, and blinked. Shane's boy? Wait—his adopted son. The boy was the biological son of Shane's best friend, a late, great NFL player. Holy, holy shit. The detective and his wife, Daisy, were going to fucking *freak*. Clay didn't know the couple as well as some of the other guys at the fire station did, but he knew that much. Any parent would.

"He'll come for you, I promise."

Keeping the pressure on the boy's shoulder, he fished his cell phone from his pocket and punched 9-1-1. After identifying himself, he gave the dispatcher a brief rundown and requested an ambulance in addition to the police who were already en route.

He ended the call, not liking Drew's pallor. He was losing blood too quickly, and they needed that ambulance *yesterday*. When the boy's eyes started to drift shut, Clay's gut clenched.

"Stay with me, Drew. Do you hear me?"

"Yes, sir." But his words were slurred, and his eyes closed despite his promise.

Biting back a curse, he kept pressure on the boy's shoulder and willed the ambulance to hurry. As he spoke to the young man in soothing tones, he wondered which station would get the assignment, but it hardly mattered. Things were going to get dicey if help didn't show up soon.

Just then, the sound of sirens cut through the air outside and relief coursed through him. Soon, he heard the bell on the door jingle and footsteps rushing inside.

"Sugarland PD," a man's voice called out.

"Back here," Clay answered.

A uniformed cop rounded the counter, weapon drawn, but he kept it at his side, assessing the situation as he moved forward. "Keep your hands where I can see them."

"I can't let up on the pressure," Clay told him. "He's losing too much blood."

The officer nodded. "Your name?" he asked, crouching on the boy's other side. He studied Drew, but kept a wary eye on Clay.

"Clay Montana. I'm a firefighter/paramedic for the city. I was walking nearby when I heard the shots, and I saw an armed man running from inside the store."

"Stick around then, we'll want to get your statement." He jerked his head at the unconscious clerk. "Any idea who he is?"

"Yeah. His name is Drew Cooper, and he's the adopted son of one of your own."

The cop cursed. "Whose kid is he?"

"Shane Ford's. He's a detective."

"Goddamn," the man said softly. "I'll go make the call."

Clay didn't envy the guy that task. As soon as the cop disappeared, Clay heard the beautiful sound of more sirens—the fire department's ambulance and truck to the rescue. In moments, there were more people hurrying into the store, and two very welcome faces appeared.

Zack Knight and Eve Tanner moved behind the counter, eyes widening when they spotted their friend and colleague kneeling next to the victim.

"Clay!" Zack exclaimed. "Are you hurt?"

"No, but this kid wasn't so lucky."

"Holy shit, that's Shane's boy," Eve whispered. "He was robbed?"

"Yeah. I was walking and heard the shots, saw the shooter run from the scene. Drew told me the man demanded his money, then shot him anyway."

Anger darkened Zack's grim expression. "I hope they catch him and nail him to the wall by the balls."

"Me, too."

Reluctantly, Clay relinquished his patient to their care and stood, grimacing at the pain. Then he stepped back out of their way, listening to his teammates discussing Drew's vitals. The young man's blood pressure was dropping.

"Let's get him out of here," Zack said.

Just as Six-Pack and Julian wheeled in a stretcher, a commotion at the door made Clay's stomach drop.

"Drew? Where's my son?"

A frantic Shane Ford burst into the store, pushing past officers and firemen. The look on his face was something Clay had seen far too many times—an expression of pure terror for his loved one. His cry of anguish when he saw Drew covered in blood, pale as death, chilled Clay all the way to his toes.

"Oh my God! Is he—" His knees threatened to buckle, and Julian was instantly at his side, holding him up.

"He's alive, and you can ride with him, okay?" Julian said soothingly.

"I—yes." The detective looked shell-shocked. "Oh God, I have to call Daisy."

The first officer stepped up and clasped Shane's shoulder. "I did that already. She'll meet you at the hospital."

Shane nodded, staring at his boy as they loaded him onto the stretcher. "Thank you."

"No problem," the cop said. "You need anything, Detective, don't hesitate to let me know."

"I will, thanks."

Clay shuddered as he watched his team wheel Drew outside. Shane never even noticed Clay standing there with blood on his hands. The man was too upset to see much of anything except his son.

Six-Pack paused on his way out and gave Clay a smile. "You did good. That boy is alive because of your quick thinking."

He thought the captain was giving him too much credit, and shrugged. "Just did what had to be done. My training kicked in when I needed it. Can't wait until I'm recovered enough to get my position back."

"You've made amazing progress. Keep it up and you'll be back before you know it." With that, the other man clapped him on the shoulder and headed out the door.

Clay's thoughts returned to Shane and his gut clenched in sympathy.

This is why I'm never having kids. I could never watch them go out the door every day not knowing if the worst would happen.

"Excuse me, are you Clay Montana?"

The woman's voice surprised him, and he turned. He'd been expecting Tonio Salvatore, Julian's brother, or perhaps one of the other detectives on the force. When he faced her, his heart lodged in his throat. By God, she was beautiful.

The redhead was regarding him with polite patience, waiting for his answer. She wasn't overly tall at around five-five or so, slender, and her fiery hair was pulled back into a serviceable ponytail. The length tumbled down her back, and he suddenly longed to free the mass from the confines of the band that held it.

Her facial features seemed almost delicate, sort of elfin, and yet her green eyes hinted at a core of steel that the strongest man wouldn't dare go against. To top it off, she was a cop. A detective, he guessed, since she wore plain clothes with her badge clipped to her belt not far from her weapon. A gorgeous little badass.

Damned if the sight wasn't arousing as fuck.

He realized she was still waiting on his response, and cleared his throat. "Yes, that's me."

"I'm Detective Melissa Ryan, Sugarland PD." Stepping forward, she pulled a small notebook and pen from her pocket, and began to write. "Did you witness the shooting?"

"Not the shooting itself," he explained. "But while I was walking, I did see the man run from the store and take off."

"What time was this?"

He thought about it. "Ten, fifteen minutes ago? Sure seemed longer than that while I was waiting for help."

"It often does." She noted the time. "He was armed?"

"Yes."

"What did he look like? Can you describe him?"

"He wasn't as tall as me, I'd say. White guy, maybe mid-thirties but that's just a guess. He was wearing jeans and a red plaid shirt. I don't know anything about guns, so I can't tell you what kind it was."

"Okay." She scribbled the information, then looked up again. A hint of something more than curiosity flickered through her gaze and was gone. "What's your occupation?"

"I'm a firefighter/paramedic for the city." With a grimace, he gestured to the cane in his hand. "Well, I'm on leave right now. Had an accident on the job and it's been a long recovery. Actually, that was my team who just left with the victim, Drew."

Her gaze softened. "I'm sorry to hear about your accident. I hope the rest of your recovery goes smoothly."

"Thanks." He gave her a smile, and she returned it. A warm feeling curled through his belly and went south. Shifting some, he hoped his attraction wasn't obvious.

As she went on, she didn't seem to notice. "Do you know the victim personally?"

"No. I just know Shane, his adopted dad, casually through some of the guys at the fire station. I've seen Drew before, but I didn't realize who he was at first."

"All right. Can I get the best phone number to contact you in case I have more questions?"

"Sure." Quickly, he recited his cell phone number and found himself praying she'd find a reason to call—and not necessarily one that involved the robbery and shooting.

She finished writing down his information and then pocketed her notebook and pen. "I'll be in touch."

I sure hope so. "Okay. I'm available pretty much anytime these days." He held her gaze, willing her to catch the double entendre.

She gave a soft laugh. "Not for much longer, I'm

sure." The sparkle in her eyes made him wonder whether she was referring to his leave, or his single status. "Take care."

"You, too, Detective."

After flashing him another smile, she turned and walked out of the store. Clay blew out a deep breath and immediately felt stupid. Kind of shallow, too. What the hell was he thinking, flirting with a cop at the scene of a terrible crime? *You're an idiot, Montana*.

After using the restroom to wash the blood off his hands, he headed outside as well, where the remaining officers had cordoned off the station with yellow crime scene tape. A shiver wracked his body. Now that the adrenaline rush was over, the crash was hitting him hard. And dammit, he still had to walk all the way home, too.

The walk started off agonizing and got worse with every step. He'd pushed too hard today and was limping badly. His left knee and hip were conspiring together, promising swift retribution for abusing them both today.

He got as far as the bus stop almost a mile in the direction of home before he had to sit on a bench. Damn, he hated to call anyone. He'd been enough of a burden to everyone already. *How the fuck am I going to get home?*

Digging his cell phone from his pocket, he contemplated his options. "Bus or Uber?" he muttered.

A honk startled him from his reverie and he nearly dropped the phone. Looking up, he saw a little blue four-door Hyundai idling at the curb right in front of him. Behind the wheel was none other than the gorgeous detective. She'd rolled down the passenger's window and leaned over to call out.

"Need a ride?"

Like you can't believe. In more ways than one.

"I don't want to be any trouble . . ."

"If it was going to put me out, I wouldn't have asked. Get in, Mr. Montana."

"Please, call me Clay. And I'm kind of stuck, so I won't refuse." Sure beat public transportation, for the company alone.

Climbing in, he buckled his seatbelt and carefully arranged his legs in the small space, hitting his bad knee once on the glove compartment. He sucked in a sharp breath but didn't make a sound of complaint.

"Sorry about the legroom, or lack of," she said, pulling away from the curb. "Adjust the seat if you need to."

"No, I'm fine. Thanks for picking me up, Detective Ryan."

"Since we're on a first-name basis, call me Melissa. And it's not a problem. I had an errand to run that brought me back in this direction anyway. Now, where to?"

He gave her his address and she nodded, turning in the direction of his neighborhood.

Melissa Ryan. The name suited her, along with the

red hair, fair coloring, and the cute smattering of freckles across her nose. Was she of Irish descent? Her last name pinged something in his memory, but he couldn't put a finger on why.

"You walked a long ways on that leg," she commented.

"Bad planning."

"What happened? If you don't mind my asking." She glanced at him briefly.

"I don't mind." He took a deep breath. "I was driving the ambulance to a call last year, crossing through an intersection, when a truck ran through his red light. I don't remember the accident, but I was told it was horrific. I almost died, and was in a coma for weeks."

"I'm so sorry," she said softly. "That must've been hell."

"It was. After I woke up, I was completely confused for the longest time, and I had no motor control. I had to relearn everything. How to walk, talk, dress, and feed myself. I'm surprised the fire department has kept me on leave instead of just giving me the golden boot."

"This city is pretty good to their employees," she said. "I'm sure they want to give you the chance to rejoin your team."

"Yeah. Every department has its limits, though. If I can't pass the physical agility test soon, they'll have no choice but to offer me a desk job or let me go." The thought made him sick. He honestly didn't know what he'd do if it came to either option.

"Well, if it's any consolation, I'd never have known you'd been through that serious an injury if you hadn't told me." She gestured to his leg. "Other than the limp, you seem to be doing really nicely."

"Thanks, that *does* help. My friends tell me all the time how great I'm doing compared to the beginning, but it's good to hear it from someone else."

"What happened to the other driver?" she asked.

Clay frowned. "Last I heard, he was sent to prison. Not for the accident, but because the police found drugs in his truck, and the possession charge violated his parole."

"That sounds like . . ." Melissa fell silent for a few moments, the strangest expression on her face.

"Sounds like what?"

"I have a cousin who was sent back to prison last year because he had an accident and the police found drugs in his truck." She shot Clay a sharp look. "Does the name *Foster Ryan* mean anything to you?"

The question was a sucker-punch right in the balls. Clay stared at her grim profile and his mouth went dry. "That's the name of the man who hit our ambulance." *And cost me a year of my life.*

"He's my cousin." She spat the word *cousin* as though ridding her mouth of a foul taste.

He gaped at the detective. "Jesus. No wonder your last name sounded familiar."

"Unfortunately, we share blood. I'd change my surname, but the cost and legalities just aren't worth it."

"I take it there's no love lost between you and him."

"To put it mildly," she snorted. But her chuckle held no real humor. "Foster and my uncle can both go to hell, but that's a story for another day. We're here. Nice house, by the way."

"I—thanks." His head was reeling from what he'd learned. This woman was related to the bastard who'd nearly taken his life. Unreal. "I appreciate the ride, too."

"It's the least I could do, considering." Her green gaze pierced him, filled with regret.

"You had nothing to do with what your cousin did. He made his own choices." Reaching out, he laid one hand over hers. "Don't take on guilt that isn't yours."

She shook her head. "I'm not, but I *am* sorry for what he did to you. I'm ashamed that he's family."

"We all have those in our family tree." He smiled, trying to lighten the mood. "That's a story for another time, too."

She gave a rueful laugh, and her eyes sparkled again. "I look forward to hearing it."

He nodded. "Thanks again."

"You're welcome."

Climbing out with his cane, he shut the door. As she backed out and started off, he cursed himself for not getting her phone number. "Dumbass."

Or was it too soon? *I look forward to hearing it.* Had she even been hinting that she wanted to see him again? Maybe, maybe not.

Exhausted, he shuffled into the house and flopped onto his couch, unable to move another step. This afternoon definitely hadn't gone as planned. He prayed Drew would recover. No young man deserved to have his life cut short when he was simply trying to do his job.

Then he thought of Melissa. Perhaps some good had come from this day after all.

In some ways, it sucked being the new cop on the block again.

Though Melissa was hardly a rookie anymore, and had made a lateral move from her previous city as a detective, she still had to endure the endless teasing. Being a cop was still very much a man's world, no matter how far the country had come with equality. The good old boy system was alive and well, and she was the lone female detective on a team of hot-blooded men.

Thank God most of them were settled down with their own wives and girlfriends. She couldn't imagine how much worse the teasing and innuendo would be if they were all single.

Being back in Sugarland was strange. She'd spent years trying to put this city and her volatile uncle behind her, and she'd thought she'd succeeded. But she'd kept tabs on him and her cousin, and their illegal operations, from afar. Like a beacon, the possibility of justice kept calling her home, and eventually she'd heeded it.

What her next move would be, she had no idea. She was here, however, and that had to count for something.

Striding into the station, she ignored catcalls and whistles from a couple of uniformed officers and kept walking straight to the area she shared with the other detectives. The guys were decidedly morose, and didn't bother to tease her when she arrived—a sign of how upset they were over the shooting.

"Has anyone heard how Drew's doing?" she asked the group.

Tonio Salvatore shook his head. "Chris called a few minutes ago. He and Taylor are doing their best to keep Shane and Daisy calm. Drew was rushed into surgery the minute he arrived at the hospital, so it's wait-and-see now."

"Guess we won't hear anything for a while."

"Probably not." The handsome, dark-haired man frowned. "I want the bastard caught who did this to that poor kid."

"That makes two of us. Want to come with me, knock on some doors, see if we can catch the perp?"

"Thought you'd never ask." He grinned. "I'm not riding in that little shit box you call a car, though. *I'll* drive."

"Suit yourself."

She followed him from the station, thinking it felt good to do something, even if they couldn't catch the shooter. Maybe they'd get lucky, though. *Who knows?*

She slid into the passenger's seat of Tonio's muscle car and covertly admired the powerful machine's interior.

"Gorgeous, isn't she?"

"Pretty cool for a penis extension."

He laughed and fired up the engine. "Now who's making sexist jokes? How come it's okay for a woman to do that and not a man? It's an annoying double standard."

Her face heated. "You're right. My apologies."

"Forget it," he said with a wink. "I was just giving you a hard time."

"But you were right."

"I usually am."

"Jesus." She rolled her eyes.

Downtown, Tonio parked at the gas station where the robbery and shooting had taken place. Other officers had spread out and searched for the perp, and questioned the locals downtown, but none had seen anything. At least none they'd found.

"They're concentrating on the more populated

areas, because that's the direction the shooter ran initially," Melissa said. "But what if he doubled back?"

"It's a good possibility. I'd want to avoid the main search area, too."

They hadn't gotten out of the car, so Tonio pulled out of the parking lot again and headed away from downtown—in the general direction of Clay's house.

As they kept their eyes peeled for anyone suspicious, Melissa's thoughts drifted to the injured firefighter. In her entire career, she'd never had such a tough time maintaining her professionalism around a witness. She wasn't sure she'd really succeeded on that score, either.

Clay was a gorgeous man. Tall and broad-shouldered, the man had blue eyes, sandy blond hair that appeared almost gold in the sun, a killer smile, and a set of dimples that had probably been the downfall of many a woman.

And there was one thing about him that made him more attractive than his looks—his determination to survive. The man was no quitter, and he hadn't spent the past year sitting around feeling sorry for himself. Hellish as the struggle must have been, Clay had pulled himself up by his bootstraps and slowly healed. She couldn't fathom how he must've felt to wake up from the coma in a body no longer under his control. To be trapped in his head, unable to speak, walk, or feed himself.

She admired nothing more than seeing his will to push on as he'd left the gas station earlier, soldiering on his way despite his obvious pain and exhaustion. The man didn't know she'd lied—there was no errand that brought her back in his direction. She'd been drawn to return, to make sure he was all right as he trudged home. When she'd seen him collapse onto the bench, visibly spent, her heart had constricted.

Thank God she'd returned. Sure, he could've called for help or waited for the bus, but it felt wrong to leave him there.

"Hey, look at that guy," Tonio said, interrupting her musings. He pointed toward a man walking along the sidewalk, hands in his pockets, shoulders hunched, head down.

"He fits the general description."

"Does it look like he's working too hard to be casual to you?"

She nodded. "Yeah. Let's see what he has to say."

Tonio caught up with the man, pulling his car alongside him, and stopped. Melissa opened the door, unsnapping the holster at her side as she got out. On the other side of the car, Tonio did the same. The subject of interest stopped in his tracks and eyed them warily, then his gaze dropped to her badge and gun.

"Sugarland PD. Where you aware there's been a robbery nearby, at the Quick-Mart?" she asked in a pleasant tone. "We'd like to ask you a couple of—"

The man took off like a turbocharged jackrabbit.

"Fuck!" she spat.

Then she bolted after him.

2

The suspect was fast, she'd give him that much.

But he was also bulkier, and that slowed his flight as she chased him through the well-kept neighborhood. She was in top shape, and he clearly wasn't. He stumbled over garbage cans and his own two feet as he began to tire.

He did, however, have desperation on his side. Perhaps a few drugs in his system as well. Determined not to be caught, he plowed ahead, heedless of her shouts to stop. Hard on his heels, she leaped over fallen debris in an alley and scaled a fence right after him, dropping on the other side and taking off again.

Where the fuck was Tonio? She hoped he was following in the car, angling for the opportunity to box in the guy, but she didn't have a second to spare a glance.

When he left the alley and leaped a resident's fence to cut through the backyard, she pushed even harder. While getting him cornered would be easier now, there was also an increased risk of his taking a hostage. She couldn't allow an innocent bystander to be hurt.

"Police, stop!" she yelled again. Not that it did any good.

The suspect tripped over a garden gnome figurine and went down hard. Instantly, Melissa was on top of his back, fighting just as hard to get him pinned as he was to throw her off. But she managed to get one arm twisted behind his back, and it was over. Quickly, she grabbed her cuffs and slapped one end around his wrist. Then she grabbed the other flailing arm and he was soon restrained, facedown on someone's lawn.

"Get off me, you piece of pig shit!" he bellowed.

"Aww, that's not very creative." She grinned, though her sides were heaving from the chase. "You can do better than that, surely?"

"Fuck you, bitch!"

"I'd say you're the one who's fucked, and not in a good way." Damn, these were the times she lived for—putting one more slimy asshole behind bars.

"You have the right to remain silent. Anything you say can and will be used against you . . ."

She finished and hauled the scumbag to his feet just as a familiar voice reached her.

"That was fucking hot, if you don't mind my saying."

Whirling, she spotted none other than Clay smiling at her from over the top of the fence, one arm casually resting on top of the slats. For a few seconds she stared at him, then snorted a laugh.

"Doesn't take much to trip your trigger, does it?" she retorted.

"A sexy lady cop tackling a bad guy in my neighbor's backyard? What's not to love?"

"Get a room," the bad guy in question muttered.

"Shut your face and get against the fence," Melissa ordered, holding firmly to his arm. Spinning him around, she pushed his chest against the boards and kicked at his ankles, urging him to spread his feet. Then she began to pat him down, searching for a weapon.

Found it, too, tucked into the waistband of his jeans at the small of his back. A wad of money was stuffed into his right front pocket, and she confiscated it as well, ignoring his bitching. Completing the search, satisfied, she tucked the gun and cash away and fished out her cell phone. Tonio answered on the second ring.

"Where are you?" he almost shouted. "Did you lose him?"

"Nope. Got him." She called to Clay, "What's your address?" After he recited it to her, she relayed it to Tonio.

"Meet you out front," he said, and disconnected.

She started to say something to Clay, but when she looked over, he was gone. "Huh. Well, let's get you off to your nice free room and board, shall we?"

This time, the perp had no comment. She led him through the gate and into the front yard, and once there, she spotted Clay coming out his own front door.

"We have to stop meeting like this, you know," he quipped.

"People will talk." She gave him a wink.

"Let 'em." He waved a hand at the suspect. "Do you need me to—"

"I'll give you a call later," she said, shaking her head. She didn't want the suspect to know Clay was a witness. Especially not since the man would know where Clay lived.

"Okay. Take care." His brow furrowed.

"You, too."

Tonio pulled up and they hustled their captive into the backseat. As the other detective drove away, she contemplated meeting the firefighter twice in one day. She might've called it fate, if she believed in that sort of thing.

She'd learned long ago to make her own destiny.

* * *

A big part of taking charge of her destiny was by putting the past behind her. But in order to do that, she was determined to find a way to take her uncle down.

Frowning, she leaned forward and studied the page on her computer screen. She was no hacker, and her attempts to probe James's finances yet again were clumsy at best.

Understandably, her limited contacts at the Bureau were reluctant to provide her with a great deal of the information they'd managed to uncover on his operation, which made her frustration worse. They didn't want her doing exactly as she was now—poking her nose in and stirring James up.

But that was what she wanted. A part of her itched for him to know she was digging, and she suspected he *did* know. Not much got by him. If she couldn't accomplish anything but being a pain in his ass, it would be worth it.

That piece of dog shit needed to suffer for the hell he'd put her through, not to mention Aunt Jennie. That could be the answer—simply piss him off to the point he got sloppy and made a move.

"Hey, Mel?"

Slowly, she looked up from her mountain of paperwork and pinned young Officer Jenkins with the laser glare of death. "My name is Melissa," she said evenly. "Not *Mel* or *Lissa*, or any other cute variation thereof."

"S-sorry," the young man stammered. "The guys told me you preferred to be called that."

She gave him a toothy smile. "Well, then they set you up."

He winced. "I didn't mean any offense."

"I know you didn't," she said with a sigh. Seemed the crew wasn't done yet with her hazing. And poor Jenk by proxy. "Anyway, what did you want?"

"Oh, um, there's a guy here to see you."

Her heart sped up. "Did you get his name?"

"It's that firefighter dude, Montana. Didn't he see your shooter earlier today?"

"He did. Thanks, Jenk."

"No prob."

Pushing out of her chair, she walked out to the lobby to meet Clay. The man was standing with his profile to her, looking out the window at the waning sunlight. Her breath hitched for a second or two. He was quite a sight to behold.

Powerful shoulders filled out his blue denim jacket, and his long legs, encased in jeans, seemed to go on forever. His straight hair covered his ears in a semi-shaggy style, the lobes just visible, and the way the strands fell into his startling blue eyes was adorable. He had a straight nose and full lips she just knew would be great at kissing.

He was leaning on his cane, and when she cleared her throat, making her presence known, he turned and gave her the full wattage of his smile.

"Detective."

"Why is it people can't use my name properly to-day?" She smiled back to let him know she was teasing.

"Sorry. Melissa." He gestured toward the back. "You called me down to have me pick the shooter out of a lineup, right?"

"If you can, though it's only a formality. Thanks to the surveillance video, not to mention the gun and money he still had on him, we've got him cold."

"I'll be glad to. Before, I wasn't sure I could pick him out, but now I can."

"How so?"

"He's got a small tattoo on the back of his neck," Clay told her. "When you turned him around to search him, I remembered seeing it when he was running from the scene. It didn't register until then."

"That'll definitely make things easier. You ready?"

"Absolutely."

She led him through the maze of desks to a hall-way in the far right corner of the next room. Down that hallway, she stopped at the fourth door and went inside, shutting it after them.

The room was dark, a curtain drawn over a long window in the wall in front of them.

"That's a two-way mirror," she explained. "When the curtain opens, they'll send in a lineup of men who look similar to our suspect. If you see him among them, tell me which one."

A knock at the door was preceded by Tonio walking inside. "Good news," he told them. "Drew is out of surgery and stable. Barring any complications, he'll make a full recovery."

"That's fantastic news!" she exclaimed.

"Sure is." Clay's smile brightened the room. "I can't imagine how relieved Shane and Daisy must be."

The young man would face his would-be killer in court, but that was certainly better than the tragedy this day could've been.

Tonio remained with them to view the suspects, and soon the curtain opened. Six men were led inside to stand against the white wall, first in profile. The men were ordered to turn in place slowly, showing both sides, their backs, and finally facing forward.

"The second one on the left," Clay said with confidence. "He's got the tattoo."

"Are you absolutely sure?" she asked. "Many people have them."

"I'm sure. This one is distinctive because of the Celtic knot design. He's also got a reddish scar on his neck underneath it right at the collar."

Pressing the intercom, she told the officer they were done, and the men started to file out. "That's it. You picked him out."

"What'll happen now?"

"He'll be bound over for trial, which may take a while to happen, but he won't see the light of day again. He has a long list of priors for burglary, robbery, and the like. But the attempted murder charge made it a whole new ball game. He's out of here."

"Good." He scowled. "I just wish Drew didn't have to face the scumbag in court."

"I was thinking the same thing."

Clay hesitated. "I was going to head to the hospital and check on him. Would you like to go with me?"

"That's very thoughtful of you," she said softly. "Yes, I'd like that."

"I'm not cleared to drive yet, so we'll have to take a cab or your car."

"I'll drive," she said. "If you can fold that tall frame into my little beer can again."

His laugh mesmerized her. "I can manage."

"I'll follow you guys," Tonio put in. "I'd like to check on Shane and Daisy, too."

Melissa collected her purse and keys from her desk, and they left the station. On the way across town, she glanced at her handsome passenger. "I didn't think you knew Drew or his family very well."

"I don't, but I feel the need to make sure he's really okay. As a paramedic, it's not often that I'm able to find out later how a patient is doing, and I happened to have a connection to this one."

She already thought he was pretty cool, and her estimation of him rose. "I feel the same."

They arrived at the hospital and the three of them walked inside together, then took the elevator up to the ICU. Once there, a nurse directed them to a waiting area, where they found Daisy curled in a chair staring at the muted TV on the wall.

Melissa liked the tall blond juvenile officer. Though Melissa hadn't worked with her much yet, she was normally all smiles at the station, so cordial to everyone she met. One look at the other woman, however, and Melissa could see she'd been crying. Her hair was disheveled, eyes red and swollen. There was a box of tissue on the table beside her, one clenched in her hand. She turned as she heard their group approach.

"Oh," she said thickly, standing. "Thank you all for coming."

Quickly, Melissa pulled her into a hug. Clay and Tonio followed suit. Once they let her go, Melissa spoke up.

"I heard Drew is going to recover. I'm so glad."

Daisy's eyes filled with fresh tears. "Thank you. We were so terrified, I can't even tell you. They said he could've bled out if a paramedic hadn't been walking by and put pressure on his wound until an ambulance could get there."

Clay looked at her and his lips curved up. "That would be me. I believe we've met before, but you may not remember me. I'm Clay Montana, and I'm happy I was in the right place at the right time."

Daisy blinked at Clay as though really seeing him for the first time. Then she cried out and the firefighter had an armful of sobbing woman. He patted her back, trying to comfort her, and gazed at Melissa and Tonio helplessly over her head.

"Shh," he said. "He's okay now."

"Oh my God! Did something happen?"

Melissa turned toward the entrance to the waiting room, where a striking, slender young man with long brown hair had halted, two Styrofoam cups in his hand. He appeared to be about nineteen or twenty, and his expression was one of pure fear. It was clear he'd misread the situation with Daisy crying.

The other woman quickly pulled away from Clay and hurried to him. "Blake, honey, no! Everything's fine. I was just thanking this man for saving Drew's life." She introduced the two. "Blake, this is Clay Montana. He's the paramedic who kept Drew from bleeding out before help arrived. Clay, this is Blake Roberts."

Blake set the cups on a table and strode over, holding out his hand. "Thank you for what you did, sir. Drew's my best friend, and I can't imagine life without him."

The older man shook his hand. "Call me Clay, and I'm glad I could help. Especially since I've been out of commission for a while." He gestured to his cane.

"I heard about the accident," the boy said. "Damn, that's some tough crap."

"Yes, it was. But I'm doing much better."

"Dude, that's great. Heard from Shane that it was a bad wreck."

"It was."

Melissa was glad he didn't go into detail—especially since it was her own worthless cousin who'd hit him and Julian that day.

Tonio looked around. "Where are Shane, Taylor, and Chris?"

"Oh, Taylor and Chris went to get a bite to eat," Blake said. "Shane is in with Drew since they'll only let one of us in at a time for ten minutes. The rest of us didn't want to leave, so they're bringing back food for us, too."

"Any chance we can visit Drew?" Melissa asked.

Daisy sighed. "Tomorrow would be better, when they move him to a regular room. Right now the ICU staff is keeping it to me, Shane, and Blake. We can only see him in shifts."

"No problem," Melissa said. "We just wanted to come by and let you all know we're thinking about you and pulling for him."

"That's incredibly sweet. When Drew wakes up, I'll let him know you were here."

"Let me know if I can do anything at all to help when Drew's released," Melissa said.

"Oh, you already have." Daisy's expression grew fierce. "You caught the bastard who shot him, and I couldn't ask for more."

"Believe me, it was my pleasure." Melissa hugged the other woman again.

Tonio stayed behind to talk with Shane, so Melissa and Clay took their leave. There wasn't much else they could do here, but the visit had seemed to mean a lot to Daisy.

Back at Melissa's car, she couldn't help but smile at Clay's struggle to fold his long frame into the front again. "If you ride with me more often, I guess I'll have to shop for a bigger car."

"I'll be driving soon, so you can ride in *my* car," he said, giving her a meaningful look.

Her heart sped up at the implication that he wanted to spend more time with her. Was that what he meant? "What kind of car do you drive? I figured you as more of a truck guy."

"A vintage Challenger. Gives me something to tinker with."

I'll give you something to tinker with. "Sounds cool. I'd love a ride sometime."

"You're on. You'll be my first passenger, soon as I get my license back." He fell silent for a moment, then asked, "Are you hungry? Can you take a dinner break?"

"Getting there. And yes, because I'm off duty now. What do you have in mind?" *He wants to spend time with me?* She felt like a giddy teenager, but pushed down her excitement.

"How about Italian? There's a nice little place close to downtown that has great food."

"I know the one. Sounds great."

A few minutes later, she parked on the street in front of the restaurant. She'd been here before, a hole in the wall that was cozy inside, not too fancy, with a fantastic menu. Her stomach growled in agreement.

They went inside, Clay leaning on his cane. He'd been on his leg a lot today, and a pang of sympathy washed through her. She didn't show it, though, sensing he wouldn't appreciate it. He didn't seem like a man to dwell on what he'd lost, but had his mind set on what would be again. She admired that more than he could know.

A hostess showed them to a booth in a quiet corner, and they took seats opposite each other. A waiter appeared, handing them both menus and promising to bring them each a glass of water while they decided, then he left them.

They both started to talk at the same time, and Clay laughed good-naturedly. "You go ahead," he said.

She smiled. "So, you've lived here all your life?"

"I have. My mother, Charlene, still lives in town, too. If it wasn't for her, I'd be in much worse shape than I am right now. She really went to bat for me after the wreck, took care of my bills and things so I didn't lose my house and car."

"She sounds wonderful," Melissa said wistfully.

"She's the best. A bit smothering at times, but a great mom."

"At least you *have* a mom."

He winced. "I'm sorry. I didn't mean to bring up any bad memories for you."

"No, no," she assured him. "I had wonderful parents, but they were killed during a home invasion when I was about six. I was in the house, but I don't remember anything about it, thank God."

"That's horrible. I'm sorry."

"It was a lifetime ago. My uncle took me in, but that wasn't the best place for me to be, so my aunt finally managed to wrest custody away from him when I was about ten. He made things so difficult for my aunt, harassing her, that she finally took me and moved away from Sugarland when I was thirteen."

"Your uncle sounds like a piece of crap, if you don't mind my saying."

"I don't mind at all because it's the truth. Uncle James is a violent man, a career criminal, and an all-around terrible person. The best thing that ever happened to me was when my aunt drove me away from his compound for the last time."

"Compound?" He brows rose in curiosity.

Just then, the waiter appeared with two glasses of water garnished with lemon wedges. "Are you ready to order?"

"Another minute?" Clay asked.

"Sure thing. Be back in a few." The waiter vanished again.

Damn. Maybe she'd said too much. Then again, might was well lay it on the table right off the bat. Let him decide if he could handle being around Melissa knowing her only family in town was a bunch of criminals led by a crazy asshole.

She continued their conversation. "Yes, a compound. Uncle James runs an illegal moonshine distillery. Quite a large and lucrative one, in fact, with a high-dollar facility. The Feds have been trying to crack the operation for years."

His eyes widened. "Moonshiners in the Tennessee hills? That shit's for real?"

"As real as that documentary on the History Channel. Watch it sometime. I did, even though I didn't need to—I lived it. This is not your stereotypical shack with a bunch of drunk, bearded men sitting around with brown jugs of shine that they make for their friends. This is a serious million-dollar business. Of course, I was so young when I went to live there, I didn't really know what they were doing was wrong. Not until much later."

"Why haven't the Feds been able to arrest them?" he asked, clearly baffled. "If it's so big, it's clearly not well hidden."

"Ah, but that's where you're wrong. It's very well hidden deep in the hills, covered by trees, and surrounded by armed guards. You think I'm shitting you?" She shook her head. "My uncle allows few people onto the property, and only when it suits him. I heard a couple of years ago that an agent tried to crack my uncle's operation from the inside and met with a grisly fate. When I used my status as a detective to check it out, I found out it was true. Many of the ones he can't kill, he buys off with bribes."

"Jesus, what a family."

"Trust me, he's not on my Christmas card list."

He chuckled. "Well, at least you're not the only one with crappy family—my dad isn't on my list, either. He left me and my mom when I was about thirteen. Just packed up and ran off with another woman one day, and never looked back. I don't even know if he's alive. Don't care."

The pain in his voice told her otherwise, but she didn't pursue the subject. "You and I, we're fortunate that we each had one great relative to care for us. My Aunt Jennie was that person for me. If it hadn't been for her intervention, there's no telling how I would've turned out."

"Was?"

"She passed away last year," Melissa told him sadly. "She had kept her house and some acreage here in Sugarland, rented it out for years. She said she wanted me to have a place to come home to, should I ever want to return. For years, I couldn't imagine ever coming back."

"But you did."

"Yeah, a few months ago. I moved in first, cleaned up the house and property. There's a small barn out back, so I fixed it up and bought a couple of horses. They're fun, and riding is an escape for me when I need it. Then I found the job at the Sugarland PD and took some shit for getting the position over them hiring someone internally. But I kept my chin up because I know I'm a good cop."

"That's awesome. You took a leap of faith then, moving home without a job."

"And then some. I just knew I had to come."

Clay studied her for a long moment, his blue gaze piercing all the way to her soul. It was like he could see inside her to the heart of her motives. "You want to bring down your uncle."

She took a deep breath. "So bad I can taste it. I don't know what I can do that the FBI can't, but I have an in they don't—Uncle James is family."

Looking worried, Clay laid a hand over the top of hers on the table. "Please, don't mess with him, or any of that. If he's as ruthless as you say, it won't matter now that you're his niece, especially when he finds out you've come home wearing a badge."

She nodded, a chill going through her. "He probably knows already. I've been a cop for years."

"All the more reason to give him a wide berth and let the government handle proving his crimes."

"I know you're right, but it's hard to let go of the idea. You have no clue how miserable I was living with him and his men."

"He didn't . . . *hurt* you, did he? Or did any of his men?" he asked cautiously.

"No, not like that. My uncle is mean, but his abuse towards me was mostly verbal. He'd hit me sometimes, which was bad enough. But none of them ever touched me sexually. Honestly, I think he would've killed anyone who tried that. Probably the only good thing I can say about him."

"Well, at least there's one thing," he muttered.

They finally studied their menus and the waiter returned to take their orders. Once they'd related their selections to him, she turned the topic toward a lighter subject.

"So, how long have you been a firefighter?"

"Nine years—well, technically eight if you count the year I've lost. I joined the fire department when I was twenty-one."

"I don't have to ask whether you love your job. You're working so hard to get back to it."

"You're right about that. I never wanted to be anything else. My lieutenant, Zack Knight, tells people he started playing with fire trucks as a little kid and never grew out of it. It was the same for me."

She grinned. "I can picture you as a little boy, zooming your fire truck all over the driveway and dreaming big dreams of driving it one day."

That got a chuckle from him. "That's pretty accurate."

Their food came eventually, and they continued to make small talk, learning about each other's likes and dislikes. They found they both loved movies, especially action-packed ones with lots of bullets and explosions. They both loved to hike, try different restaurants, and their quest for the perfect beer was a shared one.

This man is too perfect. He's so easy to talk to, and he listens.

"So, what's your worst fault?" she asked curiously. "You don't seem to have any."

"Are you kidding?" He nearly choked on his ice water. "I have plenty. I'm a bachelor, right? I leave the toilet seat up. I snore. I let my dog sleep on the couch, not that I have one right now."

"That's not a fault, that's being an animal lover," she pointed out. "That's another positive."

"Okay." He thought about it. "I procrastinate. Not at work, but at home. I forget to do laundry until I realize all my clean boxer briefs are in the hamper. So then I just go commando."

It was her turn to nearly choke. She could imagine him in a sexy pair of briefs. Even more so without them. "I don't think that counts as a fault, either. The commando part."

He laughed out loud, showing off that brilliant smile. "I'll file that for future reference."

"You do that."

His eyes locked with hers, and ooh, *the heat*. It was enough to start a fire right in the middle of the table. The connection was definitely there. The spark.

He was like a deep pool of warm water she wanted to wade into, and didn't care if she drowned. Had a man ever looked at her with such intensity? Like he wanted to learn all her secrets, peel them back one layer at a time?

"Have you ever been in a serious relationship?" he asked in a low voice.

"A couple. Neither one worked out, for different reasons. I haven't found the right person. How about you?"

"I've dated, but nothing serious," he told her.

No serious relationship in all his thirty years? She wasn't sure if that was a good thing or not.

"Uh-oh." He grinned. "You got that look on your face. I'll admit, I've been a player, and maybe a woman would view that as another fault. But a casual roll in the sheets is *not* what I'm looking for anymore."

"You get those points back, then," she teased. Silently, though, she knew that would be a deal breaker. She wouldn't put up with a man who had a revolving door on his bedroom.

Finishing their meal, they lingered for a while longer. When the waiter brought the bill, she tried to pick it up, or at least split it with Clay, but he was having none of it.

"This was my suggestion," he said firmly. "The woman does *not* pay the check for dinner. If that makes me old-fashioned, I won't apologize."

A bit of alpha male in him, then. A firefighter, a ladies' man, a gentleman. A *protector*.

Hot damn, that turned her crank on many levels.

"No apology necessary, and thank you for dinner."

"My pleasure."

The way that word rolled off his tongue made her shiver, especially with the way he was looking at her. Trying to ignore the heat rushing through her, she stood and made her way out with him at her side. She liked how he put his free hand at the small of her back as they left. It did strange, wonderful things to her insides.

As before, she drove him home—but this time with a big difference.

This time, as her car idled in his driveway, he turned in his seat to face her. Reaching out, he cupped her cheek in one big hand, leaned over, and pressed his lips to hers.

God, his mouth was soft, but with the right amount of firmness. His lips were made for kissing, his mouth for exploring. He smelled so good, too, though she couldn't place the woodsy cologne. His scent rocked her senses, combining with the heat of his touch. She wanted more, and returned his kiss hungrily, touching his face, combing her fingers through his sandy hair.

When they broke the kiss, both of them were panting and he had a serious bulge in the front of his jeans.

"My God, that was incredible," he said softly. "Can I see you again?"

"Yes. I'd like that."

What else could she possibly have said? She would

go inside with him right now if he asked. But he didn't.

"Can we exchange numbers?"

"Oh! Of course." Pulling out her cell phone, she typed in his contact as he recited it. Then he did the same.

"I'll call or text you," he said with a smile.

Another lingering kiss, and he was gone before she quite knew what had hit her.

A robbery, a life saved, a criminal behind bars, and a potential new boyfriend.

Not bad for a day's work. Not bad at all.

3

Clay awoke with a smile on his face and a better attitude than he'd possessed in months. For once, he truly looked forward to dragging his ass out of bed and facing a new day. The change had been a long time coming.

He knew who was responsible, too. A certain redhead had caught his eye and kept his undivided attention. She had beauty and brains. She was tough, too, as he'd witnessed firsthand. Watching her take down that suspect had made him so hard, he just about came in his jeans like a horny seventeen-year-old.

What was Melissa doing right now? Getting ready for work? Showering? Closing his eyes, he rolled to his back and tried to imagine her naked. It wasn't hard to picture her taut, lean body, her pale skin streaming and slick with water. Did she have a few freckles on her body that he could trace with his tongue? He sure hoped so. He prayed she'd let him.

Was the triangle at her mound as fiery as her hair? Would she be slick and hot, clasping him in a vise as he slid deep inside?

Groaning, he fisted his cock and began to pump. The hard flesh slid through his palm, sending waves of pleasure rolling through him. He imagined instead that he was slipping through the folds of her sex, pumping deep.

Moaning, she writhed underneath him, begging for more. Pert breasts tipped with pink nipples jiggled as his tempo increased. Soon he was fucking her hard, the sound of their flesh slapping together the most beautiful music he'd ever heard . . .

"Fuck!"

The curse exploded from his lips at the same moment his release shot from his cock. Creamy white ropes of cum splattered his belly and chest. He opened his eyes, heart pounding, coming down off the brief cloud of euphoria.

That had been *way* too short. His hair trigger was a sad testament to exactly how lonely his life had been the past few months. Now that his body was healing, his libido had awakened with full force. And it had a lot to do with meeting the hot lady detective.

Whistling to himself, he rose and padded carefully into the bathroom, noting that his knee and hip weren't quite as sore today. Despite his long walk the day before, he'd recovered well. That meant he really was nearly healed. His soul warmed with hope that he'd have his job back soon.

He jumped into the shower and made quick work of washing. Afterward, he toweled off and got dressed. He'd need another shower after his workout, but he couldn't exactly show up at the fire department's training facility reeking of cum.

Forcing his mind off pleasant thoughts of Melissa for the time being, he focused on the hours ahead. Firm in his resolve, he dressed in his dark blue uniform pants and fire department polo shirt. As he tucked in his shirt, he turned and stared at himself in the mirror above his dresser. Staring back at him was a man who was still a few pounds shy of the weight he'd been, but a man who was getting stronger every day.

His cheeks weren't as gaunt, his eyes less haunted than before. This man was filled with more excitement for the future than he'd been in a very long while, and it felt damned good. The clothes looked right on him, and they belonged. They were more than just clothes—they were a part of him. Something settled deep inside him and a new sense of determination steeled his backbone, along with a profound sense of peace.

*This is who I am. I won't be defeated, not at this point.
I've worked too hard to make it back, and I'm going to win.
No, I have already won.*

Slowly, he smiled. The sight of true happiness on
his own face was foreign, and awesome at the same
time. He didn't delude himself that the final lap
on the home stretch would be any less challenging
than the past year had been, but he was almost there.
He could do anything, reach any goal, now that the
end was in sight.

Eyeing his cane, which was propped against his
nightstand, he was tempted to leave it behind. While
the gesture would be satisfying and symbolic of his
attitude, it would also be pretty stupid. With a sigh,
he retrieved it. He didn't, however, use it as he made
his way to the living room.

Grudgingly, he called Uber for a ride and mentally
ticked off the days until he could get the doctor to
sign off on letting him drive again. *Two weeks.* If he
had anything to say about it, he wouldn't wait two
more days. After his time at the training facility today, he'd call and make an appointment.

His ride showed ten minutes later and he was full
of optimism as he left the house. His destination was
some twenty minutes away, on the opposite side of
town. The facility had once been a privately owned
salvage yard that boasted a run-down residence and
more than seventy acres of prime land. When the
owner had decided to sell out thirty years ago, a bid-

ding war had ensued. The City of Sugarland came out the winner, and the house and remaining junk was cleared away to birth the state-of-the art training grounds and educational center that stood there today.

The Uber driver pulled through the entrance next to a sign that declared:

LANNY C. MCBRIDE MEMORIAL TRAINING CENTER
CITY OF SUGARLAND FIRE DEPARTMENT

Clay wondered, not for the first time, what had happened to McBride and whether anyone was around who still remembered. *But for the grace of God, it could've been me on the next memorial.* The thought sobered him, and he shook off the aura of sadness that touched him every time he saw the sign.

The driveway led to a two-story red brick building with tall windows along the front. It was surrounded on three sides by a large parking lot sufficient to handle the number of firefighters and other city personnel who had business there each day. Beyond that, Clay could just get a glimpse of the track and obstacle course. Unable to be viewed from the front were several structures spread across the acreage that the department used in training drills on fighting fires.

Excitement bubbled in his blood and he itched to get out there and prove to himself that he still had what it took. Yeah, okay—and to everyone else, too.

After paying the driver, he palmed his cane and walked to the front entrance with almost no limp. The second the older firefighter behind the front desk spotted him, bushy gray eyebrows shot skyward and the man jumped to his feet.

"Montana!" he shouted, grinning from ear to ear. "How the fuck are you? And back in uniform, too. Did you get put back on duty?"

Clay suppressed a wince at the last question and smiled back, pumping the man's hand. "Jessop, you old fart! How've you been?"

"I asked you first." He crossed his arms over his broad chest.

William Jessop had been a fixture at SFD for as long as Clay could recall. He had to be nearing forty years with the department, and had given up his post at another station last year. "Let the young guys have it," he'd said back then. "I'm too old to crawl into burning buildings and hope to get out in one piece. I'm lightening my load until retirement."

Nobody had blamed him. Jessop had retained his captain's title, and now helped to run the training facility. It seemed to satisfy the older man to help the younger generation find their way within the department. He was well liked and respected by everyone Clay knew.

"I'm not official yet," Clay told him with reluctance. "I'm here to put myself through the paces and really start getting back into shape. It's time."

The captain's eyes softened with sympathy, and Clay hated that. "Do you have a doctor's note clearing you for this, son?"

"Of course I do." He nodded confidently even as he lied his ass off to a man he respected. "I just left it at home."

Jessop eyed him sagely. "Uh-huh. That's a likely story." Clay fought not to squirm as the man held his gaze for a long moment. Then Jessop sighed. "I get where you're coming from, kid. I'll give you two hours max today since it's your first day back. Keep the workout light, understand?"

"Yes, sir!" He grabbed the older man in a bear hug.

Laughing, Jessop shoved him off. "Don't make me regret this."

"I won't."

"And Montana? Welcome back."

"Thanks, Cap!"

Quickly, he signed in and hurried past the desk before the captain could change his mind. He heard the man chuckling as he turned the corner, and smiled to himself. "I'm back."

So what if it wasn't official? This was the first day of the rest of his life, and all that good shit. He planned to make the most of it.

Exiting through the back doors, he paused and took in the setup. No running on the track today. He hadn't brought running clothes and that wasn't why he was here. Next, his gaze found the obstacle course and his pulse sped up. There was his destination, and he headed for it with a determined step.

A couple of guys from Station Two were there,

running the course, working on their times. Lance, the station's captain, made the drill appear totally effortless as he sailed over walls and under fences. Climbed a tall ladder, scaled out the window of the mock house, and rappelled down again. His boots touched the ground and J.T., one of his men, whooped, pumping his fist in the air.

"Thirty-two seconds!" he called.

Lance yanked off his fire hat and grinned back. "Not bad for an old man."

"Um, Jessop is old, Cap. You're practically a kid compared to that fossil."

"I heard that, you fucking shithead!" yelled Jessop. Apparently, he'd come outside to watch the proceedings. He had his fists on his hips, feet braced apart, and looked rather menacing despite his age.

J.T. turned eight shades of red and shot the older man a smile. "I meant it from a place of love. Honestly."

"The bullshit around here is so thick today it's attracting flies."

Clay snorted and J.T. shot a pleading look at Lance. "Guess it's time to go, right, Cap?"

Lance shook his head. "Actually, I want to see what Clay's got in mind." He met Clay's eyes, his expression warm. "Welcome back. You here to run a drill or two?"

"Thanks. And yeah, I want to see how out of practice I am."

"Go ahead," Lance said, waving a hand toward the course. "We'll time you and be your spotters."

Discomfort crept over him. "That's okay. I really don't need an audience."

Jessop spoke up from beside him. "If you're not ready to be watched, you're not ready, period." His tone brooked no argument, and he didn't get one.

Damn, the old man was a freaking ninja. Frustration threatened to derail his plans altogether. He really hadn't planned on his practice being observed, but he should've known better. He knew the unwritten rule—your brothers had your back. Always. Whether you wanted them to or not. They knew he'd come back from the brink, and now that his return had been made an issue, they weren't going to budge.

"Fine," he said tersely. He handed his cane to Lance and studied the course. How many times had he run this thing? Too many to count. The route, every step, was ingrained in his memory. He had this.

"Wear these," Lance said, handing Clay his gloves.

"Thanks." Taking a deep breath to calm his nerves, he walked to the starting post, pulling on the gloves. Nodded to the group, shook out his arms and legs, and waited. J.T. shouted, "Go!"

Clay took off, sprinting for the first wall. Vaulting, he grabbed the rope and began to haul himself up. The task was harder than he remembered, and he was huffing by the time he reached the top. *But I did it!* Triumphant, he launched himself over, dangled from his fingers, and landed on his feet. His knee only gave a slight protest at being jarred, and he was off again.

Months of physical therapy had paid off. He was slower than he'd like to be, but that was to be expected. Joy surging through him, he negotiated the tire rings with ease, threw himself under fences, climbed a web of ropes. Another wall. More obstacles, until at last, the house. Quickly, he scaled the ladder and was pulling himself inside the window in seconds. He ran through the upper floor of the house, noticing a bit more twinging in his knee, but he was good.

The window on the other side of the house had a rope attached to scale down to the ground. Grabbing it, he levered himself out and started toward the ground as fast as possible. The pinch in his knee was more acute as he hit the ground this time, and he shook it off.

His friends were cheering. Smiling, he turned to face them. "How'd I do?"

"One minute, twenty-four seconds," J.T. said, peering at his stopwatch. "Not bad for your first time in a while."

"Congratulations," Jessop grumbled. "The family inside just burned to death."

The smile slid from his face and his chest grew heavy. "That's why I'm practicing, Cap," he said quietly.

"Christ, give the man a break, Jessop." Lance glared at the older man.

Jessop stood firm. "You've got to do better than that, son. A lot better before you're ready to rescue anyone."

That *was* the truth, and it hurt. But it made him even more determined to regain his former skills. "Time me again," he said to J.T.

"Sure thing."

By the end of the second run, his knee was complaining more with every step and jarring movement. He'd take some ibuprofen later, ice it, and it would be fine. But he had to keep going, no matter what.

He was sweating as he hit the ground after the second run.

"Forty-eight seconds!" J.T.'s enthusiastic yell made Clay grin.

"That's more like it. Right, Jessop?" Clay called out.

"Damned right. But you need to give that knee a rest. You're limping."

Clay shook his head. "I want to run it again with turnout gear. Load me down."

A new voice joined the group. "I don't think that's a good idea, buddy."

They turned as a unit to see Six-Pack striding toward them, his face lined with concern. "How many times have you run the course so far?"

"Twice," he told his captain. "I'm good, I swear. I improved a lot the second time. I want to see if I can equal or better my second time with all the gear on."

"I don't want you to—"

"Please, Howard?" he begged. He hated humbling

himself in front of his brothers and comrades. "I've waited long enough. This is what I am, and there's no time like the present to get my life back."

The big man hesitated, and finally relented. "All right. But if you feel the slightest bit off, you quit. I mean it."

"Sure," he said, mentally crossing his fingers.

Jessop went to fetch some practice gear while Clay made small talk with the others. When the older man finally returned, Clay studied the gear with a mixture of elation and fear. This was the true test—performing the course while being encumbered by the thick heavy pants, coat, hat, air tank, and face mask.

More than fifty pounds of extra weight dragged at him when he was finished donning the clothes and equipment. The feel was familiar, and yet heavier than he would've liked. A year ago, he'd never given the burden a second thought. The gear was as much a part of him as his own limbs. It was a sobering reminder of just how weakened he'd been.

"You okay?" Six-Pack asked, frowning.

"I'm good." The face mask muffled his words some, so he gave his friend a thumbs-up.

He walked to the starting pole, his knee really bitching now. But he wasn't about to quit. That shit was for pussies, and he was stronger than he'd been in months. He could do this.

"Go!" J.T. shouted.

He ran, legs pumping. Immediately the added strain on his body became awfully apparent. His knee was hurting in earnest now, and he felt short of breath despite the air flow through his mask. Yeah, he was out of shape, and wearing the gear highlighted that with glaring reality. Still, he refused to stop.

He barely made it over the wall, and stumbled when he dropped to the ground. Sweat was pouring down his face and temples as he ran. He struggled through the rest of the obstacles, nearly tripping on the tire rings. Distantly, he thought he heard Six-Pack shouting something, but he kept going.

The ladder on the side of the house was tough. Once he made it through the window, he started down the narrow plank path. The path had a wooden railing along the edge, creating a mock balcony. Past the railing was a sheer drop to the ground floor.

Disaster struck before he'd run three steps.

Clay's knee buckled and he fell hard into the railing, pain flaring in his ribs. The weight of the equipment threw him off-balance, pinning him to the barrier, which creaked ominously. "Shit."

Then, the wooden planks gave way with a crack that split the air. Pitched over the side, horror crystallized in Clay's brain in that split second that he went into free fall. He dropped like a stone, his one-story descent brief.

He crashed into the flooring below and agony

exploded through his back and head. On his back, he was tilted at an awkward angle, and realized he was lying on his tank. His head was throbbing, vision growing dim as the ceiling above him blurred.

"Clay! Clay, answer me!" Six-Pack boomed.

"Here," he rasped.

Heavy bootsteps raced toward him and his captain's anxious face appeared above his. "Jesus Christ. Don't move, okay?"

He moved his lips, but nothing more came out.

"Jessop!" Six-Pack called. "We need some help here!"

More footsteps clomped into the house. Someone cursed, and Clay heard Jessop speak first.

"I'll call the team from Station Four next door. We might need transport."

No hospital. Please. But he couldn't get the words out, couldn't catch his breath. Was the tank not working anymore? Everything grew fuzzier and darker around the edges, his sight shrinking to a pinpoint before disappearing altogether.

"Clay, man, stay with me." Howard's voice was calm, but Clay knew him well enough to hear the underlying panic.

"Get the mask off him," Lance barked.

Working fast, they got the device unhooked and off his face. Immediately, sweet air hit his cheeks and filled his lungs. Hands gently rolled him to the side, then removed the tank as well. The turnout coat was next, followed by the hat. A neck brace was situated around him as a precaution.

All the while they talked to him, but their voices came from far away. Too far to reach. Disappointment swept over him as the darkness closed over his head.

I failed.

"Yep, screw that little punk," Melissa said to Cori Knight with a scowl. "I hope he needs at least a dozen very painful stitches."

She was standing in the lobby of Sterling's ER, leaning on the counter talking to the nurse, who happened to be married to Zack, the lieutenant on Clay's team. She'd met new people and learned all sorts of things about how the members of the community in the city were so interconnected.

Melissa really liked the tall brunette, who was vivacious and so different from herself. Cori had once been an exotic dancer, doing so to put herself through nursing school, and had just finished up her studies when she'd met Zack. Good thing, too, because while Zack respected that Cori had gone against her wealthy brothers to forge her own way, the exotic dancing thing didn't make him too happy.

"How'd you catch him?" Cori's eyes were round.

Melissa warmed to her tale. "The punk ran into a dead-end alley. I got him cornered, then he pulled a knife. Unfortunately for him, the only thing he managed to do with it was cut himself when I took his stupid ass to the ground."

Cori laughed. "And here you are, waiting for him to get fixed up before you cart him off."

"Right you are. He's already under arrest for boosting car stereos. And oh, yeah—assaulting a police officer. That's gonna cost him."

The suspect was in the exam room with a uniformed officer keeping watch. That was fine with Melissa. She'd rather be out here talking to Cori than back there listening to that punk-ass kid spouting about police brutality and how he was going to sue the department for injuring him.

By restraining him and causing him to get cut with his own knife. Which he'd intended to use *to kill an officer*. What the fuck ever. Some people were so stupid, they'd buy into that "poor criminal" shit.

A commotion outside the entrance caught their attention, and she turned to see a team of firefighters coming through the door. They were pushing a gurney with their patient on it, faces grim, upset clearly showing in their eyes.

Melissa recognized the biggest one from the scene of Drew Cooper's shooting at the gas station. The other two, an older man and a younger one, she didn't know.

"Oh no!" Cori hurried forward in distress, toward the patient.

Melissa spotted the sandy blond hair of the man

on the gurney, and her heart lodged in her throat. "Clay?"

"Training accident out at the McBride Center," Captain Paxton was telling Cori. "He fell one story and landed on his back. Possible head injury. Vitals are stable, but he lost consciousness before we left and hasn't come to."

Melissa's hand went to her mouth and she stared, helpless, as they rushed past her, through the double doors leading to the trauma rooms. She hesitated only a couple of seconds before she followed. Nobody stopped her, probably assuming she had official business. Which she did, just not with their newest patient.

Lingering in the doorway to the room they'd taken Clay, she watched as they cut off his polo shirt. Hooked him to all sorts of monitors. He'd already had in IV in place, so they transferred the bag to the hospital staff, who hung it on a silver stand.

"Pupils are reactive," another nurse said.

"Pulse and blood pressure are good."

A tall doctor strode past Melissa into the room, taking over. After examining Clay for a few moments, he nodded. "He's stable. I don't see evidence of broken bones or internal bleeding, but I'm ordering a CT scan of his head and torso to be sure. He should be awake by now."

"There's a lump back here, Doctor," Cori told him, pointing to the area. She looked at Paxton. "Concussion. Was he wearing his fire hat?"

"Yes, and it probably kept him from busting his head open. Still, this is the last thing he needs after recovering from a profound head injury this past year."

The doctor's gaze sharpened. "Oh? Tell me about that."

Amazingly, the doc seemed to be the only one around who hadn't heard of Clay's accident and recovery. After the big captain gave him the short version, the doctor frowned. "We're making his CT priority. Bump whoever is scheduled next and get Mr. Montana in there, stat."

"Yes, Doctor." Cori hurried out to do as he ordered.

Melissa felt sick. How the hell had Clay managed to fall one story during a training exercise? Who the fuck was supposed to be looking out for him? She wanted answers, and she was going to get them one way or another.

She stood there until they rolled Clay past to take him for the CT scan. She got a good look at him, and she hated that he was so pale and still. So vulnerable.

He'd come so far in his recovery, only to have this happen. *God, please let him be all right.* She didn't know him, really, or why he was suddenly so important to her. But he was.

And she wasn't going to rest until she knew he was out of the woods.

* * *

Oh my fucking God!

Every square inch of his body felt like it had been beaten by hammers. And backed over by a semi truck for good measure. Taking stock, he knew where he was. He was intimately familiar with this position, and he'd never wanted to be back here so soon. Or at all, though that wasn't realistic thinking for a firefighter.

Hurt, during a training drill. During what was supposed to be his successful debut to get back into his job. *Way to go, shithead. I'm sure Six-Pack was real impressed.*

Footsteps entered the room, approaching his bed. With an effort, he opened his eyes and blinked in surprise. Melissa was there, hovering over him. She looked worried, too, and that knowledge warmed something inside him—and embarrassed the crap out of him.

"Melissa," he said, attempting to sit up. "What are you doing here?"

"I was here earlier getting a perp stitched up when you were brought in." She took a seat next to him and laid a hand on his arm. "Got him carted off to jail, and I'm back to check on you. How do you feel?"

He considered that. "My head throbs. All the way to my feet. Yeah, I'm one big ball of aches and pains."

"I heard you fell. What happened?"

His face heated in humiliation. "I'd like to claim I was saving someone, or something cool. I just over-did it at the training center. I got tired from running the drill, and the last time I was in full gear. I was jogging through the mock house when my knee buckled. I crashed into the railing and fell over the balcony to the first floor. Landed on my back and hit my head."

Her green gaze darkened. "You were damned lucky you didn't break anything."

"Did they already examine me?"

"Yeah. You've been out for an hour or so, according to your captain. He's really worried, by the way. I'll send him in."

He caught her wrist when she went to stand. "Wait. Not yet, okay? I'd like to talk to you a bit longer."

"Sure." One corner of her mouth tilted upward.

He wanted to kiss the spot. Right there, where her smile started. He wanted to see the excitement on her face grow. *Damn it, I can't get hard in the middle of the ER.* "So, when are they springing me?"

"Not so fast. There was talk of keeping you tonight for observation. It would serve you right for scaring everyone."

"Oh, hell no. I've spent enough time in this place. I'm not staying here overnight."

"You'll stay as long as the doc says you have to," Six-Pack said in his deep voice. The scowl on his face was ominous as he walked into the room and stood at the foot of Clay's bed.

"Cap, I'm not—"

"This is not a discussion." The anger on his face was palpable.

"Um, I'm going to let you guys have some quality time." Melissa stood, shooting Clay a look of sympathy. "I'll talk to you later."

"Counting on it." He gave her a crooked smile, wishing she didn't have to go. After giving his arm a squeeze, she headed out. But not before turning and giving him a wink behind Howard's back.

"What's going on with you two?" the captain asked, taking her vacated seat.

"I'm not sure just yet," he admitted. "I know I'm going to ask her out. She's a fine woman."

The big man made a noise of agreement. "She seems to be. But I'm not here to talk about your love life."

A sinking feeling settled in his gut, and he braced himself for whatever his captain and friend was going to say.

4

"You're an idiot," Six-Pack began.

Clay stared at his captain, wishing the bed would swallow him whole. That wasn't exactly what he'd expected the man to say, even if it was true. "Howard—"

"But I'm an even bigger one for allowing you to push yourself too hard, too fast." He fell silent for a moment, studying Clay intensely, as if he could see all the way to his soul. He probably could. "Here's what's going to happen. You're going to continue the training drills until you're back into shape and ready for duty. And you'll do it under my direct supervision."

He couldn't help but bristle some. "Look, I know I fucked up today, but I don't need a babysitter. I—"

"This is nonnegotiable, Clay. I'm *not* babysitting you, count on that. Your stamina isn't back up to speed, and you could've been killed. That would've been on my head as much as yours, and believe me when I say I never would've gotten over it."

Clay's gut clenched, and he knew Six-Pack was right. For all the man's tough exterior, he was a nurturer at heart. The captain was solid gold, as good as they came, and losing a man on his watch would destroy him.

"I'm sorry, Cap," he said contritely. "I didn't mean to be reckless, I swear. I was just feeling so high after my first and second runs went so well. I ignored my body's signals that I was done for the day, and I paid. It won't happen again."

The captain's face softened. "I know it won't, because I'll be there to make sure it doesn't. We'll get you on the roster again, but we'll do it safely."

"What's the plan?"

The bigger man thought about that. "You and I are going to work out together when I'm not on shift. We'll run, do weights, exercise. Not too heavy at first, but build up gradually. We'll run the drills each day until you can do them in your sleep without breaking much of a sweat, just like before."

"You really believe in me," he said quietly.

"I always have. Don't doubt that for one second. I

knew when you came out of the coma and turned the corner for the better, nothing would stop you. I like being right." A smile curved his lips.

"Thanks, Cap. Coming from you, that really means the world to me."

"I mean it. You've got what it takes to make it all the way back, and I'm going to be with you every step of the way. We'll get started as soon as you're out of here and cleared to work out."

"You got it."

Six-Pack held out his hand, and Clay shook it. The captain said good-bye and left Clay to his thoughts, which were bouncing around in his head like Ping-Pong balls. Howard didn't say shit he didn't mean, and that was a huge comfort to Clay. There was real hope, and he clung to it with all he had.

His goals were in sight. He just had to stay the course, not give up.

Nothing worth having is ever easy. Isn't that how the saying went? It had sure proven true in his case. *Easy* was a word that had been stricken from his vocabulary long ago. Fortunately, he'd risen from the ashes and removed the word *surrender* from it as well.

"Are you trying to send me to an early grave?"

Clay glanced at the doorway and suppressed a groan. Who the actual fuck had called his mother? When he found out who was to blame, he'd skin them alive. "Hey, Mom."

"Don't you *Hey, Mom* me." Despite her huff, he saw

the very real strain in her eyes and around her mouth. "What in the ever-loving hell are you doing in the ER? And are you wearing . . . turnout gear?" Her eyes narrowed.

Shit. He swallowed with difficulty as she moved to stand by the bed, glaring down at him. His mouth was dry as cotton. "Well, um, I was running some drills at the training center, getting back into shape, and I may have pushed a little too hard."

"Oh, Clay."

Her eyes softened, a hint of moisture making them shine, and guilt speared his gut. He'd caused his mother no end of worry and heartache for months.

"I'm sorry for scaring you. Again."

She took his hand. "That seems to be the tune life is playin' for us lately. When Howard called, he said you fell, but he didn't mention how it happened. I should've known you were out there pushing yourself over the limit."

Dammit, Cap. Way to throw me under the bus.

"I want my life back. I've worked damned hard to make it happen, and I'm not going to stop now that success is in reach. Is that so wrong?" He tried to keep the edge out of his tone. Tried to suppress the old hurt that rose whenever he picked up on his mother's doubt. He knew her misgivings stemmed from the stress of his injury and recovery, that she didn't mean to discount his efforts to rejoin his team—but it still slid under his skin like a barb.

"Of course not, baby. Nobody wants that more for you than me."

"But?"

"I won't lie—I'm scared," she admitted, perching on the chair next to him. Her blue eyes, so like his, were haunted. "I'm so damned afraid for you to go back to work."

There. She'd said it. His formidable mother had voiced her fear, something she rarely did. He studied her, this still-attractive woman with a core of steel who'd struggled to be both father and mother after his dad had left them. This lioness who'd fought every battle for her son to make sure he had a good home, a happy childhood.

She'd been through personal hell while Clay was growing up, made huge sacrifices to make ends meet. This was a woman who didn't scare easily. But the truth was, the wreck and following months had taken their toll on his champion.

"Mom, I was driving through a green light," he said gently. "I just happened to be on the job when that guy in the truck ran his red light. That sort of accident can, and does, happen to people every day. I—"

She held up a hand to forestall his argument. "I realize that. Believe me, I've heard it from everyone. It's an irrational fear, but it's mine and I'm working on it. Now, tell me how you fell."

Keeping it brief, he related the story. When he was

done, his mother's face was white as a sheet of paper. "You fell from the second story? Right onto your back? Jesus Christ, Clayton! What if you'd hit your head?"

"Um . . ." Apparently Six-Pack hadn't enlightened her on that part.

"Oh my God," she moaned. For a second, he thought she might fall out of her chair in a dead faint. "You can't afford another head injury, son. You know that."

"I know, but I'm fine. It was just a bump, not a big deal." She saw right through his lie with those laser-sharp eyes of hers. He hurried on to distract her from that line of questioning. "Anyway, I should be out of here soon."

"Who's going to watch over you tonight?" she pressed. "There's no way you're staying alone, not with a concussion." Clearly, she was having none of his bullshit.

I love my mom. I really do. But I can't take any more of her hovering over me like I'm going to keel over dead any second. I'm done.

A knock at the door caught their attention, a timely interruption that no doubt prevented what could have been a heated argument. His mother turned to greet the visitor and Clay looked over to see a head of burnished red hair pop around the corner.

"Hey, Clay, I thought I'd—" Melissa stopped short

and flashed a contrite smile. "Oh, I'm sorry. I didn't realize you had more company. I'll come back later."

Charlene's face brightened and morphed into an expression Clay knew all too well. *Uh-oh.*

"Nonsense! I'm not company, I'm Clay's mother. Come on in! I'm sure he'd rather have a pretty visitor at his side than his old lady here harassing him about being more careful."

Appearing a bit hesitant, Melissa stepped inside. "Well, if you're sure . . ."

"Definitely." As Melissa came to stand on the other side of the bed, his mom showed no signs of leaving. Instead, she eyed the newcomer curiously. "I'm Charlene Montana."

"Melissa Ryan," she said, returning the other woman's scrutiny in a polite, friendly way.

"So, how do you know my son?"

Always to the point, his mom. Clay sighed. Both women ignored him.

"We met on an armed robbery call yesterday. I'm the detective the department sent to investigate the case. Clay's my star witness."

"What?" His mother's eyes grew wide, and her voice rose as she snapped her sharp gaze to her son. "You were in the middle of an *armed robbery* this week and you didn't think to tell me?"

So not what he wanted his mother to learn about, today of all days.

"That's not exactly how it happened," he replied, trying to soothe her ruffled feathers. "I was out for a walk and I heard some popping sounds, then I saw a man run from inside the store at the gas station downtown. I wasn't actually inside when it went down."

"Thank goodness." Charlene's hand came to rest over her heart as if to hold it inside her chest. "Was anyone hurt?"

Melissa picked up the story. "A young clerk was shot in the shoulder, but he's going to be fine. The boy is a senior at the high school and is the adopted son of a detective I work with."

Sympathy etched his mother's features. "I can imagine how frantic your friend must've been, and how relieved he is now that the boy is going to be okay," she said with feeling. "I know what it's like to be on the receiving end of that type of phone call."

"Shane, my detective friend, and his family are beyond grateful that Drew is healing. And I caught the suspect, so he's up on attempted murder charges as well as the robbery. He's going away for quite a while."

"Good. I hope they throw away the key," his mother said with a satisfied nod.

"I'm sure they will, since it's far from his first offense."

His mom cocked her head and said thoughtfully, "That explains how you met, but not why you're here now. Have you two become friends? Or something more, since you're making hospital visits to your witness—"

"Mom," Clay interrupted, mortified. "Melissa and I are getting to know each other. We just met."

"Melissa? Not *Detective Ryan*? Hmm."

There was a sparkle in her gaze and a smirk on her face that said she knew what was going on. Really, it wasn't too hard to figure out, and she was obviously delighted by the prospect that her love 'em and leave 'em son had an interest in someone.

Covering his embarrassment, he looked at Melissa and was glad she seemed to be completely unaffected by Charlene's prodding.

"Well, I have to go," his mother said, standing. "I just remembered I have a piano lesson to teach in an hour and I have a stop to make before I head home."

"Don't go on my account," Melissa began.

She smiled. "I'm not, no worries." She smiled and turned to Clay, and bent to give him a kiss. "Take care of yourself, son. If they let you go tonight, promise me you'll let someone watch over you."

"I promise," he murmured. "They won't release me unless I do, anyways."

"Nice to meet you," Charlene said warmly to the detective.

"You, too."

Then she took her leave faster than Clay had ever seen her do, especially since he'd been hurt. He shook his head and made sure she had time to move well out of earshot before he spoke.

"Sorry about Mom. She's like a dog with a bone when it comes to my life and everyone in it. Sometimes I think she lives vicariously through me."

"Hey, it's not a problem." Melissa gave him a warm smile as she sat beside him. "Don't all parents do that?"

"I wouldn't know. Never had the urge to find out what parents go through."

"You don't want kids?"

He shrugged, then winced at the ache the movement caused. "I don't know. Maybe. I'd like to think I'd be a much better father than mine ever was."

"I'm sure you would be, with an awesome mom like yours as a role model."

"Thanks. Though I'd have a lot to live up to where she's concerned."

"You really love your mom. I can hear it in your voice, and see it in your face. Even if she annoys you." Her grin was infectious.

"Picked up on that, did you? I sure hope she didn't."

"I'm sure she did. Moms have superpowers. Besides, they annoy us on purpose like it's their supreme goal in life."

He laughed at that. "True." After pausing a beat, he said, "I'm glad you came back. And not just because I think you're beautiful."

She flushed at that and glanced away, but he saw the pleasure on her face.

"Thank you. And why's that?" she asked, looking back at him.

"I enjoy your company," he said truthfully. "I like being around you . . . and I feel drawn to you."

"I feel the same way." Her voice was quiet, lips curved upward. "So, what do we do about this?"

"Let me take you to dinner? Not tonight, obviously. But soon, like this weekend?"

"I'd love that."

She beamed at him, and his heart stuttered. God, he wanted her. "Anywhere in particular you love? Or don't love?"

"I'm not that picky. Anything pretty much, except Indian. I'm not a fan of curry."

"Done. I'll call you in the next day or two."

"Sounds good. In the meantime, we need to get you sprung from this place."

He grimaced. "The doctor may keep me, especially since I don't want to bother anyone to watch me overnight."

"Even if that someone is me?"

Whoa. He blinked at her, not sure how he felt about being her responsibility. Being under her care. All night. *Well, one part of me knows exactly how it feels about the idea.*

"I couldn't ask that of you."

"You're not asking. I'm volunteering." She snorted.

"Like it would be a real hardship to watch over a sexy fireman all night. Besides, it's either me or your mother."

"Well, when you put it that way." They shared a smirk, and he wondered just how much sleeping would be involved. Surely his body wasn't in *that* much pain from his fall.

Slow down, horn dog. That kind of thinking is why you're still alone. Think with your big head for a change.

"Good. Let me go find the doc and see if we can get you out of here anytime soon."

With a wink, she disappeared and he settled back to wait. He was wading into unfamiliar territory. Maybe he was getting in over his head by testing out having a real relationship when he had no clue what he was doing.

But it didn't feel that way. This felt good, and right. So what if she wasn't a supermodel? She was beautiful to him and possessed a down-to-earth quality he'd never come across before in anyone he'd been with. She was tough. Smart. She made him hard as a rock every time he saw her.

Shit, I have it bad.

Heaving an exasperated sigh, he willed his erection to subside before Melissa came back with the doc. Yeah, that was a humiliation he could do without.

With this woman, he was determined to be a gentleman. This could be a really, really long night.

* * *

Melissa found the tall, older doctor who'd treated Clay upon his arrival and persuaded him to come take another look at his patient and consider releasing him. It hadn't been too difficult, since the ER had gotten busy and Clay was taking up a bed they could use. They either needed to admit him or let him go.

If the doc realized Melissa was more than just a cop to the injured firefighter, he didn't let on. She figured he must know, though, because she was certainly acting more like a worried girlfriend than a professional.

Girlfriend. That had a nice ring to it, especially where one sex-o-licious man was concerned. She told herself not to count her chickens, but there was no mistaking they shared a connection. One with real potential.

She trailed the doc into Clay's room and watched as the man checked her fireman's vitals and reflexes.

"On a scale of one to ten, how's the pain?" the doctor asked.

"About a six."

The older man arched a brow. "You either have a high pain tolerance or you're downplaying how much you hurt."

"Um, maybe it's more like an eight. But I'm fine, really."

The doctor hummed and used a light to check Clay's

pupils. "Reactive, which is good. But you're still concussed, and I want you off your feet and resting for a day or so. You're going to be more sore tomorrow than you are today, and that will slow you down a bit."

"Great," Clay muttered.

"Don't complain. You've apparently got nine lives, so someone up there must be looking out for you even if you've used two of them already."

"Sorry, Doc. I'm just tired of being laid up."

"I understand, believe me. I had a motorcycle wreck about fifteen years ago, almost got myself killed. I know all about long recoveries and the frustrations that come with them."

"Jesus, I'm sorry to hear that. But I'm glad you're okay."

"Me, too." He patted Clay gently on the shoulder. "Tell you what. I'll release you as long as someone can keep an eye on you tonight."

Clay's relief and happiness were palpable as he smiled at the doc. "Thanks! I'll be good, I promise. And my friend here is taking care of me."

The doc's eyes twinkled as he glanced between them. "Well, I'd feel better already if I were you."

"Trust me, I do."

Melissa blushed as the doc went on.

"Any nausea, dizziness, confusion, or any combination of those, I want to see you back here immediately."

"Yes, sir."

"Fine. I'll have a nurse draw up your papers, then you're free to go." He held out a hand and Clay shook it. "Take care, and I hope the next time we meet, it isn't here."

"I couldn't agree more."

The doctor took his leave, and in less than half an hour, Clay was released and being wheeled out the door. Melissa had to admit he was a good sport about the treatment, but then, he was probably used to it given his trials of the past year.

"Wait here, I'll get my car."

She laughed at his groan regarding her vehicle. She figured he was developing a real dislike for her little car, a suspicion that was proven correct as the nurse stuffed him into the front passenger's seat.

"Damn. If I spend much more time with you, I swear to God I'll buy you a bigger ride. I wouldn't let you refuse, either, because it would totally be a selfish gift."

"Who says I'd refuse? While you're splurging, make it an SUV the size of a small yacht with bigger balls than yours."

Clay barked a surprised laugh and then winced in pain. Humor shone in his blue eyes as he glanced at her. "I can't believe the things you say sometimes."

"Too much?"

"Nope. You're just yourself, and I really like that about you."

"Good. Because I couldn't change if I wanted to.

I'm a cop and I work with a bunch of men. A woman learns to roll with their humor and all that testosterone or she gets run over. Simple truth."

"You're right," he said. "We have a woman on our team—Eve Tanner. Firefighting is a predominantly male job because most women simply aren't strong enough to pass the physical agility portion of the test. That's not being sexist, it's just a fact."

Melissa nodded as she pulled out onto the street. "Believe me, I know. And that's how it should be when it comes to placing a person's safety in the hands of a first responder." She was passionate about that subject.

"Yeah, some people cry and get all precious about making the tests easier for women. Let those people get trapped in a burning building and then get stuck with the firefighter who was admitted to the department based on their sex but can't carry them down a ladder before they burn to death, and they'll stop their squawking soon enough." He snorted before he continued.

"Anyway, I'll admit I've never given much thought to how hard it must've been for Eve to fit in with us. She's strong and savvy, yet she has to prove herself every day in a way the rest of us don't. It's hardly fair."

A tendril of jealousy slithered through Melissa, which came as a surprise. She wasn't the jealous type. The way she saw it, any man you had to worry about wasn't worth the effort. What she was feeling for Clay was different, though. His good heart shone through every little thing he did. She sensed he wasn't a man to stray once he'd made his choice. No, the niggle of the green monster was a pure base reaction, and she hated not being able to completely suppress it as the question popped out of her mouth.

"So, is Eve married?" *That wasn't obvious or anything.*

The man's sexy lips curved upward. "Very. She's married to my former captain, who was promoted to battalion chief last year. They're so in love I could go into a sugar coma every time I'm in the same room with them both. Of course, that's true about all the guys on my team and their main squeezes."

She couldn't help but laugh. "Main squeezes?"

"Whatever. They've gone from a group of independent, beer-drinking, womanizing he-men to a bunch of lovesick fools gushing about china patterns, babies, and new furniture." He shuddered. "No, thanks."

And yet, here you are with me, knowing I don't do one-night stands. Interesting.

She kept her smile to herself as she drove them to his house. If he wanted to cling to the last of his fading bachelorhood like it was a life preserver, fine. She'd let him, and wait him out. Then he wouldn't know what hit him.

At his house, she pulled into the drive and parked, then walked around to the passenger's side to help him out. He was having none of it, though, and waved her off when he stood and she tried to steady him.

"Stubborn," she said, rolling her eyes. "If you fall on your butt, don't blame me."

"I won't. I've already done that, thank you very much. No repeats."

She did, however, carry the turnout pants he'd been wearing over his work trousers. True to his word, he stayed on his feet all the way to the front door. Fumbling with his keys, he let them inside and exhaled a breath of relief.

"Well, that was fun."

"I'll take your word for it." She studied his tired face. "Are you hungry? We could go see what I can throw together. You need to have something before you take any more pain meds."

He nodded. "I could eat. There's plenty of stuff to throw together. I can help—"

"Not a chance. I want you to grab a shower if you can manage it, then come on out and I'll have something ready."

He appeared hesitant at first, but relented. "Okay. I can negotiate the shower by myself. I really appreciate this. I mean, you don't even know me that well." Moving closer, he reached out and touched her face.

Her skin warmed where his fingers brushed her cheek, and she smiled. "It's not a problem. With any luck, I'll get to know you a lot better."

"Oh, I don't think we'll need any luck."

Closing the space between them, he took her mouth. His lips were as perfect as she remembered, full, soft, with just the right amount of firmness. She cupped his jaw as he delved his tongue between her lips, and she loved the feel of his day-old scruff. The strength of his body pressing into her. His manly scent, some woodsy aftershave paired with good, clean sweat.

The man fired all her blood cells, made her purr like nobody else ever had. The few men she'd dated, even the couple she'd gotten serious with, had never made her putty in their hands. She wanted Clay to do whatever he desired, longed to give up control. She'd waited forever, it seemed, to find a man she could trust with her body and heart, and something told her this man could be the one.

When he finally broke the kiss, the evidence of his arousal was pressed hard against her through his pants. He was breathing like he'd run a race, pupils dilated, naked lust on his face.

"I'd better get that shower," he said quietly. "A cold one."

She stepped out of his space and stammered, "I-I'll see to the food."

Flashing a grin, he turned and made his way carefully toward a hallway off the living room where she assumed the bedrooms were. Heaving a breath to calm her raging libido, she walked into the kitchen and started rummaging around for something to make for dinner.

A package of fresh, uncooked chicken tenders sat on the shelf in the fridge. Taking them out, she placed them on the counter, then went in search of inspiration in the pantry for how to fix them. Bread crumbs and garlic—perfect.

Soon, she had the chicken coated and pan-frying in olive oil, and the delicious aroma started to fill the kitchen. Next, she got out a package of wild rice and set it aside to cook when the chicken was close to being done.

A loud crash and sharp curse reached her ears. Setting the pan of chicken off the fire, she turned off the burner and dashed toward the bedrooms, heart pounding. More cursing led her to the last bedroom on the right, which was apparently Clay's room.

The man was leaning against a mahogany dresser like his life depended on it, one arm wrapped around his bare torso. He was wearing nothing except a dark blue towel around his lean hips, and her mouth dried up.

Despite the bruises starting to purple his ribs, the man was a study in panty-melting pleasure. His broad chest was smooth, stomach flat and taut with nice definition, his legs long and toned. He looked like he could stand to gain a few pounds yet, but if she hadn't known about his accident, it never would have been evident to her.

Oh, he'd recovered nicely.

Snapping herself out of it, she studied his pained expression in concern. "Are you all right?"

"I'm fine," he ground out, appearing embarrassed. "I stumbled and ran into the damned dresser, knocked half the stuff off it, and hit my sore ribs."

"Sit down," she ordered, pointing to his king-size bed.

"I said I'm okay."

"Sit down!"

"Jeez, you don't have to yell at the injured guy," he muttered. But he did as he was told, parking his fine ass on the bed.

Trying to ignore the way the towel was riding high on his thighs, she walked over and bent to examine his ribs. There was a red mark on his side where he'd banged into the dresser, perhaps the corner, but he seemed all right otherwise.

"You have to be more careful," she murmured, placing a hand on his thigh.

He sucked in a breath. "Right now, I think it's you who needs to be careful."

The part of the towel covering his lap rose, giving proof to his words. Lips quirking up, he leaned back on the bed until he was resting on his elbows gazing up at her, blue eyes mesmerizing.

"You make a man forget where it hurts—well, almost."

She licked her lips in anticipation, their dinner forgotten for the moment. "Anything I can do to speed along your recovery?"

Giving her a smoldering look from under his lashes, he said, "I thought you'd never ask."

Then he reached for the towel secured at his hip, and flung it aside.

5

With the gauntlet thrown down, so to speak, she stared at the perfection spread before her. She must've been quiet a bit too long, because he started to appear worried.

"Too much?" he asked, echoing her earlier words.

"Not at all. You're beautiful."

"Men aren't beautiful," he protested.

"Most aren't, but you are." Tentatively, she laid a hand on his thigh again and began to skim slowly upward.

His eyes darkened, and he didn't voice a counter-argument as she continued her exploration. He merely watched, desire suffusing his features. His skin was warm, supple, but when she finally reached the place where his inner thigh met his groin, he was hot as a firecracker.

His long, thick cock was curved toward his flat belly, and his large balls were nestled underneath, drawn up tight. The head was weeping pre-cum, and suddenly she'd never wanted anything more than to taste him.

Sitting on the bed beside him, she scooted closer and palmed his sack, squeezing and rolling his balls. She liked how this earned an immediate groan of pleasure, and it encouraged her to continue. Next, she wrapped her hand around his length and began to stroke gently, down to the root, then to the tip. Again and again, taking satisfaction in how his eyes rolled in growing ecstasy and his hips began to thrust into her touch.

When she bent and sucked the thick head between her lips, she thought he'd launch himself to the ceiling.

"Melissa," he breathed. "My God."

She loved the reverent sound of her name on his lips. The way he seemed so captivated by the attention she was lavishing on him. Encouraged, she took him deeper, sucking, making him wet and slick. He moaned, burying a hand in her hair, gently guiding himself deeper, but not forcing himself too far.

Good thing, because she couldn't take all of him. He enjoyed her efforts, though, and so did she. The simple act of savoring his body, making him writhe, made her sex heat and filled her with need. She continued to savor him, sucking and stroking, until he gently pushed her back.

"I want to make love to you," he rasped.

"You're hurt, and you shouldn't exert yourself that much."

"I won't if I stay on my back and you ride me." He arched a brow, his gaze stoking the flames inside her even higher.

"That is a very tempting proposition," she said.

"Only tempting, or irresistible?"

His infectious grin brought out her playful side even more. "What do you think?"

With that, she sat up and rid herself of her plain, unattractive polo she'd worn to work, yanking it over her head and tossing it off the side of the bed. Next, she reached behind her and unhooked her bra, then let it slide down her arms and off. It joined the polo.

"Now look who's beautiful," Clay breathed. Reaching out, he grazed one nipple, bringing it to a peak.

She leaned into his touch, encouraging more, and he cupped the breast carefully, kneading the pillowy flesh. A moan escaped her lips as he tweaked the nipple, sending little shards of electricity all through her.

"How long has it been since someone worshipped you, baby?" he asked softly.

"I can't say anyone ever has," she admitted.

"But you've had lovers, surely."

"Yes, but I can honestly say nobody's ever made me feel special."

"Let me see what I can do to change that."

She had a feeling he wasn't just talking about tonight. The idea thrilled her, and frightened her a bit, too, but she decided to let herself go. To trust that maybe, finally, she'd found someone she connected with who was ready to go the distance. To take all her hopes and dreams and nurture them into reality.

He played with her breasts, lavishing them with attention until his hands drifted downward, his fingers settling on the button of her pants. She knew what he wanted without asking, and was all for it. Quickly, she kicked off her shoes, shed the pants, sliding her panties off with them and kicking them to the floor.

Rolling to his side, he leaned on one elbow and splayed one big hand on her belly. He studied her naked body with a hunger that no man had ever shown, his palm skimming down to her nest of curls, where he hesitated. In silent encouragement she parted her thighs and his exploration continued until he found her sex and slipped his fingers between the folds.

She gasped as he stroked inside, tending a desire that had gone neglected for far too long. Not just the desire for sex, but for human touch. Connection. The validation that she was a woman and not just cop.

That she was a sensual creature with much to offer the man bold enough to take her.

His deft fingers worked her channel, making sure to graze her clit, hitting that sweet spot just so and with a delicious rhythm. Soon she was wet and hot, clinging to his arm and begging.

"I'm ready! Let me ride you, please!"

His chuckle rumbled next to her and he situated himself on his back again, the look he gave her with those gorgeous blue eyes nearly making her come on the spot. Quickly, he reached into a drawer in the nightstand, found a small packet, ripped it open, and sheathed himself. She wasted no time climbing aboard, straddling his lap. Then she brought the head of his cock to her opening and sank onto him.

"Oh, shit! Baby," he said hoarsely. Gripping her waist, he began to pump her up and down, sliding out, then filling her again and again.

And God, how he filled her! The man had a lot to be proud of, and he knew how to use it. Even flat on his back, injured, he knew exactly how to please his partner to the point where she was nearly mindless.

They established a tempo, Melissa bouncing on his lap, the fires flaring higher and higher. She braced her hands on his chest, loving the feel of his hard muscle under her palms, flexing as he drove into her. His sandy blond hair was fanned around him, making a halo around his handsome face. He had eyes only for her, and didn't break their gaze for a moment.

She felt like he was seeing all the way into her soul, and the moment was so profound she wanted to laugh and cry at the same time, with pure joy. *I think he's the one. The man I've been waiting for.*

Whether he felt the same remained to be seen.

All too soon, she went over the edge. With a cry, she spasmed around his length as he stiffened with a shout, finding his own release. One arm came around her, pulling her down, and he kissed her fiercely, devouring her mouth like a starving man.

Finally they broke apart and he said, "You take my breath away."

"Same here. I can't believe I'm still conscious." She studied his flushed face. "Are you okay? In any pain?"

He grinned. "You just took care of the most important ache."

"I'm trying to be serious." But she smiled to take the edge off her worry.

"Every muscle is letting me know I fell one story and landed on my back," he admitted. "I think I'll skip my workout tomorrow."

"You think? Shit, I'm lying right on top of you!" Hastily, she moved off him and snuggled into his side. "I'm sorry."

"No worries, baby." He kissed her temple and

wrapped an arm around her, urging her to lay her head on his chest.

She obliged, starting to settle in—and then remembered something important. "Crap, I forgot about dinner. I set it off the burner when I came to check on the noise in here."

"It's okay. We can finish it after our nap, and if it's not salvageable, we'll order in."

She yawned. "Sounds great to me."

I don't think he's the one—I know he is.

With that thought, she drifted into a contented sleep, safe in his arms.

Dinner was saved. Any semblance of rest later that night, however, wasn't happening.

Melissa took her duty to watch over him quite seriously, and she dutifully woke him every two hours to make sure he had no lasting complications from his accident. The last time she roused him, around four in the morning, he'd assured her that if he didn't get some real sleep, he'd knock himself out on purpose.

Thank God she'd decided he wasn't going to die and finally let him crash.

Stretching, he grimaced at the protest in his sore, stiff body. That fall had really done a number on him, and he knew he was damned lucky not to have been killed. Then he rolled and checked the time on his cell phone—almost ten a.m. His new lover's body was curled up next to him, a living furnace. He liked the closeness, a lot.

It occurred to him that she should've been at work by now, and he hoped she wasn't going to be in trouble because of him. Rolling to his side, he studied her face, relaxed and innocent in sleep. Anyone who could see her now would never believe the tough core of steel she possessed, or that she dealt with the darker side of humanity on a daily basis.

She appeared delicate, her skin pale and all that red hair falling around her. Freckles on her nose and shoulder that he wanted to trace dotted her porcelain complexion, making her seem younger than she was.

Thinking back to their lovemaking the night before, he couldn't help but grin. Melissa was just as passionate and sexy a lover as he'd known she would be, and he couldn't wait to explore other facets of this woman he was becoming enamored with.

Her lashes fluttered and suddenly he found himself looking into a pair of enormous green eyes. "Morning," he said, kissing her on her cute nose.

"Morning." Her sleepy smile tugged at his heart.

"Aren't you supposed to be at work?"

"Why?" She stretched. "Want me out of your hair?"

"No way! I just don't want you to be in trouble with your captain."

"I won't be. I called in yesterday and took a personal day. I wanted to be sure you were all right, and I didn't want to leave you here alone."

"Well, I wouldn't really have been alone, but you saved me from being smothered by my mom."

"You say that like it's a bad thing," she teased. "Your mother is great."

"Yes, she is. But she and I have lived in each other's back pockets for the better part of a year, and trust me when I say we both need our space. She appreciates her recent freedom as much as me, though she'd never admit it."

"My aunt never would have, either. She loved me so much, and as a kid I didn't know just how much of her freedom she sacrificed for me. Oh, *she* didn't see it as a sacrifice, but later I realized that was technically true. She took in a young girl and raised her with love, and never once complained. In fact, she embraced loving me."

"Who wouldn't?" he said softly. He was afraid he'd crossed a line too early, but his lover merely smiled.

"Thanks. There were days I tried her patience, though. Along with the confidence she gave me came my stubborn nature, my ability to assert myself. It got me in trouble more than once as I found my path."

"You? In trouble? I can't imagine that."

"Ha! My early teens were hell on the poor woman. I snuck out of the house, smoked, drank, spray-painted buildings, whatever I could to prove I was a badass." She paused. "Looking back, I know now that I was simply testing my aunt's love for me."

"You wanted to know whether she'd stick around and love you anyways," he guessed softly.

"Exactly. When I realized that her faith in me and her love would never waver no matter what I did, I settled down. Started to figure out what I really wanted in life. And that was to help other people, maybe save someone from the James Ryan of their world."

"That's a worthy goal, and I'd say you're doing a fine job."

She flushed at the praise. "Thank you."

Reaching out, he cupped a hand behind her head and pulled her in, brushing his lips against hers. Then he took the kiss deeper, dueling his tongue with hers, drinking up her taste as if it was rich, red wine. Being with her sure made him feel like he'd been drinking, with all of the great highs and none of the inconvenient loss of control.

"Wanna jump in the shower with me?" he whispered into her mouth. "I'll make it worth your while."

"You don't have to bribe me, sexy. You had me at *wanna*."

"Really? What if I said, 'Wanna go on a five-mile hike?' What then?"

"You'd have to present a bigger challenge. I could do that in my sleep."

"Ten miles?"

"Warmer."

"Wanna go eat fried rattlesnake nuggets?"

"Um, no. That's where I draw the line." She narrowed her eyes at him playfully. "You haven't eaten them, either."

"No, but I wanted to see if you had."

She shook her head. "Come on, weirdo, let's get that shower."

"Hey! I was sexy a minute ago."

"Don't pout. It makes me want to do sinful things to your body."

Clay pouted harder, sticking out his bottom lip, and she laughed as they got out of bed. He stood carefully, taking stock of his injuries.

"How are you feeling?" she asked in concern.

"I'll live, because death doesn't hurt this much. Trust me, I know."

"That's not even remotely funny." Skirting the bed, she went to him and took his hand, expression sober.

"Sorry," he said, contrite. "I've had a while to come to terms with the accident. It's either make jokes or cry, and I've done enough grieving over what happened to me. Come on."

Tugging on her hand, he led her into his bathroom. Once there, she made him turn around so she could examine his back.

"Damn, you're black and blue back here."

Turning around, he craned his head to look at the area in the mirror. He could definitely see where he'd landed on the air tank. "Looks like I was pelted by giant watermelons. Feels like it, too."

"Poor baby. Let's get you warm, I'm sure that will help."

"Oh, I'm sure it will." She snickered at his double entendre.

He turned on the water and let it get hot.

Shutting the stall door behind her, his lover stepped into his arms. He pulled her close again and reveled in the sensation of his naked skin against hers. Her taut ass felt damned good in his palms, perfectly round and smooth. His lips descended, warm and soft, searching. His tongue licked the roof of her mouth, behind her teeth, probed everywhere, because he wanted to learn every ridge.

Then his hand worked between them, fingers combing through her curls to locate her clit. She widened her stance, encouraging him to continue. He played, stroked, and teased, sending little tingles to her limbs that he felt vibrating against him, and he loved that he was responsible. Unable to resist, she wormed her hand between them as well and cupped his heavy sac, testing its weight.

He broke the kiss, groaning. "That's it, baby. Explore all you want. That belongs to you."

She seemed to like that idea, a lot. "Really, all for me?"

"No one but you."

He was serious about that, and he hoped she believed him. Hell, he'd never been this hung up on a woman before, and this time he didn't want to fuck and run. *I want her.*

The unwanted image of another man fucking her came to the fore, and he ruthlessly squashed it. She was with him now, and he'd give her every reason to stay.

He spread his legs wider, making it clear she could do what she wanted and he'd enjoy every second. Carefully, she knelt and grasped the base of his cock with one hand and steadied herself by holding onto his thigh with the other. Looking down, he admired how the water cascaded over her head, wetting her hair, and streamed down her breasts and stomach. She was a redheaded water goddess come to life. *And she's mine.*

Testing the seeping head of his penis with her tongue, she made a happy noise. "Sweet," she said. "I love doing this, especially to you."

"Not as much as I love you doing it."

She sucked on the spongy crown, smiling up at the way he melted under her ministrations, making incomprehensible noises that might've been endearments. Or curses. Who knew? All he cared about was that she was rendering him incapable of speech.

She took him down her throat, loving that his entire length, her mouth the perfect sheath, warm and slick. She laved every vein and contour, eating him like a stick of candy. He was putty in her hands and mouth, so she upped the ante, increasing the suction on his cock. He fisted a hand in her hair and he increased his rhythm until his hips were snapping like a piston, fucking her face like there was no tomorrow.

She opened to him, squeezing his balls, apparently trying to make him lose control. Her efforts met with resounding success. After giving a series of quick thrusts, his body tensed, balls drawing up tight.

"Fuck! I'm coming!"

He tried to pull out, but she held fast to her prize. Surrendering to her wishes, he came with a shout, his seed spurting hot and thick onto her tongue, down her throat. She drank him greedily, seemingly not wanting to miss a drop, though it wasn't easy. He was loaded with cream and hadn't enjoyed this in quite a while.

When he slumped against the tile, she licked away the last drops, then let him slip from her lips and smiled up into his sated face. "Damn, you taste good, handsome."

"Thanks." He grinned. "I'll bet you taste even better right now. Can I find out?"

"The second we get done."

Taking her hand, he helped her to her feet and then took great pleasure in soaping her all over. The soreness in his body was all but forgotten in the wake of his orgasm, and playing with her under the spray was the best medicine he could've taken.

After their shower, they got out and he dried them both off. She glowed under the attention, and he vowed to do it more often. When they were done, he led her back into the bedroom, where he hoped he could rise to the occasion one more time. He wasn't a teenager anymore, but damned if she didn't make him feel like one.

"Come here," he said in a low voice.

Face flushed with the heat from the shower, and perhaps from the heat between them as well, she moved into his arms.

He pulled her close, nuzzled into her neck. His teeth scraped along her vulnerable skin, and he let her feel his canines, nipping at her flesh. God, that was a huge turn-on. Her moan heightened his anticipation as he continued downward, pausing to capture a pert nipple in his teeth.

She squirmed, buried her fingers in his hair, and tugged. He chuckled, sucking and teasing the nub, giving the tiniest shock of pain with the pleasure, then repeated his attentions on the other. Then he knelt and kissed a line down the middle of her stomach, pausing where her patch of neat curls began.

Pushing her thighs apart, he rubbed her slit with two fingers. Spread the moisture, looking his fill. The hunger on her gorgeous face made him feel ten feet tall. Sexy. Excited. So many things he'd been unaccustomed to in the past few months. Had he ever been this happy and fulfilled? Not even close. This was different, and extraordinary.

Bending, he tasted her, and a growl of male approval rumbled in his chest. "So sweet. I'm getting spoiled, being able to taste you like I want. Make love to you."

"What about your back—"

"It'll be fine. Nothing matters but this."

Damned straight. No amount of bruising could match the heat of his desire. Nothing could compare to the warm, strong woman who writhed above him as his tongue worked its magic, laving slowly, sending the most delightful shivers to her nerve endings. Then he worked between her folds, licking her core. Taking his time, driving her insane. Finally, she pulled at him, almost frantic.

"I need you inside me! Protection?"

"To be honest, we don't need it on my account," he said huskily, pulling her onto the bed. He helped her get settled, then moved up her body to position himself between her legs. "I was tested in the hospital, and I haven't been with anyone since. But it's your call."

"I haven't been with anyone, either. Not in ages. I'm on birth control and I've been tested, too."

"Then can we do without?" He grinned. "I want to feel you with no barriers between us."

"Yes, I'd love that," she said, face alight with anticipation.

He sealed the deal with a searing kiss, easing the head of his cock inside her, blowing his own thoughts to dust. Then he slid deep, his girth stretching her but not enough to hurt, filling her, knowing he was more complete than he'd ever been.

Being inside his lover, fucking her with no latex between them, was mind-blowing. He'd never allowed himself to fuck a partner bare, and shit, he'd been missing out! She clung to him, palms spread on his back, then she seemed to remember his injuries and loosened her hold. But she stroked him gently, as though she wanted to love away the pain. As far as he was concerned, she could kiss each bruise and make it disappear.

His thrusts gained in power and he held on tight, gasping in enjoyment as she licked the salty skin of his chest, sucked at his collarbone. She pulled back a bit to watch his face, lips slightly parted, expression steeped in bliss. Glorious red hair curtained her face and she made such a sexy picture, it drove him to the edge.

"Oh!" she breathed. "I'm going to come!"

"Do it, baby," he rasped. "Come on my cock!"

The last of his control snapped and the orgasm swept him in a rush of heady ecstasy. She followed him over, clutched him tightly, crying out as he shouted, emptying his hot seed. Filling her to overflowing. When their spasms died, he eased to the side, slipping out of her, and gathered her close. With a contented sigh, she rested her head on his chest and wrapped an arm around his middle.

"You were wonderful," she praised.

"So were you, sweetheart. That was everything I've wanted, and more." He kissed the top of her head. "I never knew what I was missing."

He heard a sniffle, and her arm tightened around him.

"Me, either," she said softly.

They dozed for a while, not a care in the world.

If only he'd known their idyll wouldn't last.

Three days later, and he was ready to get back into his workouts and practice. Lazing around, making love with Melissa whenever she wasn't working, was awesome, no doubt about that. But he had a job to do and he wasn't going to waste one more second getting back to it.

He bugged his captain so much with calls and texts, the big man finally broke down and relented, starting their drills a few days sooner than he'd originally planned. That was great by Clay.

True to his word, Howard started him out at a slow but steady pace. Each day the captain was able to get free, they met at the training center. If he was on shift and the team had no calls, the rest of the guys would join them. They'd run a couple of miles around the track, then proceed to the weight room for a light to medium workout. After that, they'd run the obstacle courses and other drills until Clay could do them without breathing hard.

The only one they hadn't yet tackled by the time the next two weeks had passed was the model house.

Everything else went smoothly, and the team was proud of him. They said so. Hell, Clay was proud of himself. A few months ago, he hadn't been able to walk or feed himself. And now?

"Thanks to you guys and your faith in me, I'm getting myself back where I need to be," Clay told them one day after their drills. "You don't know what that means to me."

"Shit," Zack said, shaking his head. "You would stand by any of us, am I right?"

"Damned right."

"That's just what we do," Julian put in, clapping Clay on the shoulder. "A team sticks together."

"I think this calls for a celebration," Six-Pack declared with a smile. "I propose we have a cookout at my place next Saturday with our boy here as the guest of honor. After all, it's not every day a guy gets told, 'Welcome back to the team.'"

"A cookout sounds—" Clay stared at his beaming captain, then the rest of them who were chortling and elbowing each other like fools. "Wait. Does that mean what I think it means?"

"You bet." The captain stuck out his hand. "Welcome back, Clay. I'll expect you to report for duty Monday at seven a.m. sharp. If you want your spot back, that is."

"Oh my God. Yes! Yes, I'll be there!"

A cheer went up, and Clay pumped Howard's hand vigorously. Then he found himself being slapped and hugged by his friends, who were almost as happy as he was. Even Jamie, always so quiet, joined in the fun wearing the biggest smile Clay had ever seen on him.

Clay turned back to the captain. "I've still got to pass the physical agility test."

"Just a formality. We've all seen what you can do, and I don't have any doubts you'll pass with flying colors. Just keep up your workouts."

What a rush. He could hardly catch his breath at the prospect of rejoining his team.

"Hey, I may be bringing a date," he told them when things had calmed down. That brought the expected good-natured comments and whistles.

Six-Pack looked smug. "A certain pretty lady detective, I assume?"

"You assume correct. I have to ask her, but I'm pretty sure she'll come—if she's off duty."

"Things are progressing well, then?"

"They are. I think she's the one, man." Kissing noises ensued from all around him. "Shut up, assholes," he said with a laugh. "Every one of you is so pussy-whipped, you can't even get a beer after work without permission."

A few grumbles of agreement rose up, except one.

"I'm not pussy-whipped and probably won't ever

be," Jamie said, almost to himself. Then his face flushed when he seemed to realize Clay had heard his comment, and he glanced away shyly. "I mean, I'm still single."

Clay patted his arm, wondering what that was all about. "No rush, my friend. She could be just around any corner."

Clay could've sworn he heard the younger man mutter, "Not likely," before they headed out together as a group. Oh—did Jamie swing the other way? If so, he didn't have to worry about coming out. None of the guys would care.

The mystery was soon forgotten as he bade the guys good-bye. He was flying high as a kite, and needed to tell someone his good news. His mother deserved to be the one to hear it first, because she was the one who'd been through hell with him.

Briefly, he thought of calling, but decided this was best delivered in person. On the way, he stopped at the grocery store on impulse and picked up a small gift for his mother. Once he arrived at her house, he hurried up the steps, marveling again that he was able to do so. He rang the doorbell and waited.

A few seconds later, he heard footsteps. Then the door opened, and his mom's face broke into a huge smile at seeing him there.

"Clay! Are those for me?"

Stepping inside, he drew her into a big hug and spun her around, the flowers clutched at her back.

He laughed as she squealed, then he set her down again. "Yes, they most certainly are!"

"Oh, thank you! I haven't gotten flowers in ages." Taking them from him, she sniffed the blooms in appreciation. "What's the occasion?"

"They're a simple thank-you from me, for sticking by me all these months. You deserve much more, but I don't have a million dollars lying around."

She smiled. "I'll take the flowers. But I sense there's much more to your visit."

"What makes you say that?" He was going for casual, but failed.

"Because you're practically radiating happiness that's so bright it's about to blind me. What gives?"

Taking him by the arm, she led him into the living room, where she urged him to sit on the sofa. She perched herself beside him, set the flowers on the coffee table, and waited.

Taking a deep breath, he told her, "I got back my position on the team. I start on Monday."

For a few heartbeats she just stared at him, and his heart sank some. What if she wasn't happy for him? What if her fears were too great to allow her to move on? He needn't have worried.

Tears moistened her eyes, and her genuine smile was as bright as he felt. "Oh, son. I'm so happy for you. You've come such a long way, and you've worked so hard. Congratulations."

Then his mother gathered him into her arms and

hugged the crap out of him. For a few moments they stayed like that, while he enjoyed the simple comfort and support only a mother could give. And his mother soaked up the reassurance from him in return. That he was a capable man, and could take care of himself. That she would let go of her fears, for his sake.

"Thank you," he said hoarsely. "For everything."

"You're my son, and the light of my life. I wouldn't have been anywhere other than by your side, fighting for you."

That was the final piece he'd needed to complete his new lease on life. What every man wanted and needed—the love and approval of his mother.

They wound up in the kitchen, talking and eating fresh-baked chocolate chip cookies as she put the flowers in a vase and made them coffee. They talked about a bit of everything that day, including Melissa.

"You going to tell your young lady the good news?"

"You bet, as soon as I leave here."

"She's pretty special, isn't she?" Her expression was open, curious.

"Yes, she is." He took a deep breath. "I'm falling for her, Mom. I think she's it for me."

"If so, I'm happy for you," she said with a wistful smile. "I knew one day a special woman would come along and steal your heart."

"But no woman could ever take me away from

you." He scooped her into a hug. "You'll always be my number one."

"Oh, I don't think so," she said with a chuckle. "But I love you for saying so."

"I love you, Mom."

"And I love you, my baby."

That wonderful afternoon would remain one of his favorite memories, always.

The day his life came full circle, and began again.

6

Melissa was at her desk poring over a case file when Shane walked into the room the detectives shared and called out to her.

"Hey, someone's here to see you. Says he's here to lodge a formal complaint."

"Aren't they all?" she muttered, shooting her friend a dark look. "Tell him to fuck off."

In the next instant, her tall, sexy firefighter filled the doorway. "Now, is that any way to talk to your man? You really want me to scram?"

Standing, she came around the desk, ignoring the ribald comments of her fellow detectives. "Absolutely not. Unless you really do have a complaint, in which case you can—"

"My only complaint is I'm not getting enough time with you this week, sweetheart."

"Aww," Taylor drawled from the corner. "Ain't that the sweetest thing ever? I'm turning diabetic over here."

Melissa shot him a glare. "Shut up, dickface. How many times have you texted Cara today? Don't think I didn't see that kissy-face emoji you sent her when I walked by, either."

Shane grinned at his partner. "She's got a point."

"You're right," Taylor sighed, winking at Melissa. "Guess we're all a bunch of lovesick idiots around here."

Clay changed the subject as he addressed Shane. "How's Drew?"

Leaning against his desk, Shane said, "Physically, he's doing great, considering. He spent almost a week in the hospital, then he was released. Ended up having some nerve damage in the shoulder, so he's been doing physical therapy. He hasn't been back to work yet, and I'm not sure he will. The nightmares are getting to him, worse than when he first came to live with me after his dad died."

"I'm sorry to hear about the nightmares, but I'm glad he's healing."

Shane nodded in acknowledgment. "So how are you holding up? Still working out at the training center? Melissa told us about it."

"Actually, that's what I came here to speak to her about." He turned to smile at her. "I've got some great news, but I may as well tell everybody at once. I start back at Station Five on Monday. I've got my team back!"

"Oh! That's wonderful!" She took him in a fierce hug, and his arms came around her. After a quick, chaste kiss on the lips, she stepped back and grinned at him. "I know how much you've wanted this and how hard you've been working for it."

She wanted to give him a better, deeper kiss and do some real celebrating. But that would have to wait until later.

"It's so surreal," Clay said, chest puffed out with pride. "I was running drills with the guys earlier, and Six-Pack sprung it on me. They all knew and were waiting for him to tell me. It was fantastic."

"I'll bet," Shane said, sticking his hand out. "Congrats, you deserve it."

"Thanks." They shook and then Clay turned to Melissa. "When are you done for the day? I was thinking we could get some dinner."

"I'm about ready to wrap up, and I'm starving. That sounds great."

"Why don't I wait for you and I'll drive us. I can bring you back to your car later."

"It's a plan." She smiled at him, then her eyes widened. "You're driving again?"

"Yep, got the all-clear for that, too. I'm totally independent again."

"That's great! I'm so happy for you." She bussed another kiss on his lips. "Give me just a few minutes and I'll be right out."

"Okay, baby. Shane, Taylor, good to see you."

"You, too," they chorused.

As soon as Clay was gone, Shane's face broke into a shit-eating grin. "Baby?" This, immediately followed by kissing noises from Taylor.

"Shut up, man. You're both dicks."

"The teasing just means we love you," Taylor said happily.

"I'd hate to see how you treat someone you loathe."

They just laughed, knowing she didn't take her own words seriously. It was all part of bonding with the guys—taking their shit on a daily basis.

"I'll say this, at least none of you give me shit because I'm a woman."

"Nope," Shane said. "We're equal opportunity dickheads."

"That's a comfort."

Shaking her head, she finished her paperwork and shut down the computer. Once her desk was tidied, she said good-bye to the guys and headed out. She found Clay waiting in the lobby and they walked out together.

She couldn't help but admire his tall, strong build, his long legs encased in jeans that hugged his ass just so. In the few weeks they'd known each other, he'd filled out in all the right places, put on more muscle. He no longer appeared as though he'd been out of commission for a prolonged period of time, but was fit and healthy. His shoulders and chest strained against his button-up shirt, and his sandy hair fell around his handsome face in artful disarray.

All in all, her panties were about to go up in flames. With any luck, her lover would put them out. She smiled to herself at the stupid analogy, but it didn't stop her from wanting it to be true.

"What are you smiling about?" he asked, taking her hand. "You look like the cat who swallowed the proverbial canary."

"Oh, I was just thinking how I'd rather we have each other for dinner."

He shot her a look full of lust, his gaze darkening. "How about dessert?"

"I can handle that."

He drove them to a new Mexican restaurant on the outskirts of town, and they chatted companionably, holding hands. After a few minutes, however, she began to notice that he was looking in his rearview mirror an awful lot, his expression increasingly tense.

"What's wrong?" Her body went on alert.

"I could swear that SUV has been following us since we left the station. He's made every turn I have. Could be my imagination, though."

"Could be." But his words gave her a chill. Especially when she looked in the mirror as well and spotted the vehicle a couple of cars back, hanging behind them instead of passing to go with the flow of faster traffic.

As he made the final turn onto the street where the restaurant was located, the SUV turned in a different direction and they both relaxed.

"Guess I'm just paranoid, huh?"

"No," she said. "Never hurts to be cautious." She was aware that her uncle couldn't be happy that she was back. As a cop, no less, one who was still checking into his business at every opportunity.

During the weeks Clay had been working with his captain to get his spot back on the team, she hadn't been idle. She'd been scouring the Internet for any information on James she could get. She'd even used one contact at the FBI to dig up some dirt on her uncle's money flow, though more details were needed on exactly how much was in his accounts, records of purchasing his supplies, and such. She was jabbing a stick at the snarling bear.

It was possible he'd stoop to scare tactics to get to her—such as having her followed and not really bothering to hide it. But she didn't want to bring him up and put a damper on their evening.

Inside, they were shown to a table in the corner. Immediately, a server brought a basket of chips and a bowl of salsa large enough to feed a small army.

After ordering a beer for Clay and a margarita for her, they dove in and discovered both the chips and the salsa were very good. A few minutes later, they'd decided to share a double order of chicken fajitas and were enjoying their drinks while they waited for the food.

"I like this place," Clay said, looking around. "Good so far, and not too kitschy."

"Me, too." She saluted him with her margarita. "Great choice."

They talked about this and that until the food came, and then they dug in with enthusiasm. The meal was every bit as delicious as the aromas suggested, and they got their fill while they talked.

"So, my team is throwing me a welcome back party at Howard's house this Saturday, and I'd like you to go with me, if you want."

"I'd love to. I want to get to know your friends and their wives and girlfriends." Slowly, she was being introduced to his world, and she loved that he wanted her there.

"It's a plan, then."

"Should I bring anything?"

"Not as far as food. The guys will have so much we'll never be able to eat it all. If you have a favorite beer or hard stuff you like in particular, you can bring it. But I wouldn't even worry about that if you don't want to, because there's usually enough booze at our shindigs to fill a lake."

She laughed. "Got it. Do we need to take a taxi or Uber?"

"Nah. I drink, but not to excess, especially after the accident." He tapped the side of his head with a finger. "Can't afford to lose any more brain cells."

"Wise decision. Though I hate that you've had to make allowances for things that most people take for granted."

"It is what it is." He shrugged. "Can't change anything. In truth, the two good things that have come out of this whole mess is that it brought me and my mom closer than ever, and I met you."

"Me?" she asked in surprise. "How do you figure your accident caused us to meet?"

"If I hadn't been recovering and out of work, I never would've gone for that walk downtown the day the gas station was robbed. I never would've met you."

"And you wouldn't have been around to save Drew. That's three good things."

"True." His eyes were warm.

"I love that you're a *glass is half full* kind of guy."

"I try. I'll admit, this last year hasn't been easy when it comes to maintaining a positive attitude."

"You're human. Anyone in your position would have trouble spreading fairy dust and unicorn farts."

He nearly choked on his beer laughing. "God, don't do that! I never know what's going to come out of your pretty mouth."

"Sorry. The guys I work with, it's all their fault."

"Uh-huh." Clearly, he didn't believe her.

They finished their dinner, talking companionably until it was time to leave. Clay snagged the check and refused to let her pay even part of it, saying it was his invite. He agreed she could get the next one, though, so she was content.

As they drove back to the station to get her car, she found herself searching for the SUV that had trailed them before. She saw no sign of it and soon it was all but forgotten.

Clay pulled up beside her car and put his into park. "Come to my place?"

"I'd love to. But I do have to get up for work in the morning, so I'd have to leave early to swing by home and get ready."

"I have an idea. How about I follow you home, then you get some clothes for tomorrow. Leave your car there and I'll drive you to my place, then to work in the morning."

Excitement buzzed through her. "That sounds great, but that's a lot of driving for you, plus you'd have to get up early."

"I don't mind, especially since it gives me more time with you. And I need to get used to getting up in the mornings again anyway. Monday's going to be a bit of a culture shock."

She smiled. "Well, if you're sure."

"I am."

He gave her a toe-curling kiss and then she reluctantly parted from him and went to her own car, sliding behind the wheel. She pulled out of the parking lot, Clay following, and hummed to herself. Life was just about perfect right now.

Which was why it came as an unpleasant surprise to see a dark SUV following a couple of car lengths behind Clay. There was no way to tell if it was the same one, since it had no distinguishing features, but the sight was enough to unnerve her. *Were* they being paranoid? Since she'd been back in Sugarland, she'd received no direct contact from her uncle, threats or otherwise.

Had he learned that she'd been discreetly poking around in his business? Perhaps she was starting to piss him off. She knew she should leave the digging up to the Feds, but the need to bring him down was a living thing under her skin.

It struck her that perhaps her uncle felt exactly the same way.

Once again, the SUV dropped off and was nowhere to be seen by the time she reached her house. Parking her car in the driveway, she went inside with Clay to pack some things in her duffel. She tried to work fast, but it wasn't easy with her sexy man pressed to her back and nuzzling kisses into her neck.

"Clay!" She giggled, tossing in a shirt for work. "I'll never get this done if you don't stop."

"Sure you will. Eventually."

More nuzzling. Laughing, she wiggled out of his embrace and finished packing, sticking her tongue out when he pouted at her. Just as she was ready to go, she snapped her fingers. "Dang, I forgot about the horses. I need to feed them real quick."

"I'm finally going to get to meet them?" He brightened at that. "Are they broke?"

"I have three, and yes, they are. Do you like to ride?"

"I do, but I haven't been in ages," he said with enthusiasm. "Think we could go riding sometime?"

"You bet." She was glad he liked horses, because she didn't have any intention of giving them up. They were her big babies. "Let's go and I'll introduce you."

They took her bag to his car first, then she led them around the side of the house to the barn that sat a short distance away, in the back. As usual for this time in the evening, the trio was already waiting near the breezeway to the barn, ever hopeful for their grain. Upon spotting her, they nickered softly in greeting and began pacing back and forth.

"They're gorgeous," Clay said. "How long have you had them?"

"I got them right after I returned to town and moved in. They're rescues from the SPCA. Their previous owner had nearly starved them to death, and I nursed them back to health."

"Poor things. I can never understand how people can be cruel to helpless animals. Why have them if they can't afford to take care of them?"

"Good question. I wanted to strangle whoever was responsible the first time I laid eyes on them. These three are as gentle as lambs and love people, even after what was done to them."

They stood at the fence for a few minutes, letting Clay get acquainted with her equine friends. The threesome—two brown and white mares and a dappled-gray gelding—sniffed her lover curiously, and stood still for the scratching he gave them on their necks and ears.

The genuine smile of delight he wore as he spoiled them struck a cord deep in her heart. Her aunt always claimed you could tell the color of a man's soul by the way he treated his mother, women in general, children, and animals.

Clay Montana was the total package. A real man among men.

"Come on, let's get these big lugs fed." Turning, she opened a side door on the barn that led to a raised feeding area and stepped up. "This is where I keep the feed bins and hay. This area is separated from the rest of the barn and has those holes cut in the wall over their feed troughs so I can dole out the food without actually getting into the stalls with them."

"That's pretty convenient." He smiled at the sight

of the three horses lined up in their individual stalls, noses poking through their cutout squares in the wall. They were all nickering as if they couldn't wait another second to eat.

"It is. Makes getting the job done quick and efficient."

"Do they stay locked in their stalls at night?"

"Not typically. They like the freedom to roam, and they're smart enough to come back inside if the weather gets bad."

"What about predators?" He frowned in concern.

"I suppose you've never seen a horse run a full-grown coyote or large dog out of his stall," she said, chuckling. "Believe me, nothing we have around here is going to bother them."

"Well, that's good." He appeared relieved.

"I'd only lock them up at night if there was a problem of some kind, like a rash of horse theft in the area or teenagers getting up to mischief." *Or my uncle, threatening what's mine.* But she didn't say so. "You ready to go?"

"Whenever you are."

But as soon as she had the door to the feed room shut, she found herself spun around and trapped against the side of the barn by one very big, horny fireman.

"What are you doing?"

"If you need an explanation, I'm obviously doing

something wrong." Pushing her back even harder against the side of the barn, he grinned and cupped her face. "You game? Nobody's going to see us out here."

Before she could voice a protest, he crushed his mouth to hers. Licked inside to play with her tongue, and she loved his essence. He tasted of beer and something else potent that was all Clay. Skimming his palms downward, he found the edge of her shirt and journeyed underneath, finding the mounds of her breasts.

"I've been dying to touch you all day," he said quietly.

She moaned, arching into his touch, giving him permission to keep going. Her bra was gone in an instant, and he enjoyed plucking her nipples, teasing them to taut peaks. Then his fingers found the button of her pants, making short work of that and the zipper.

His hand slipped inside her panties, sought her silky curls. Brushed through them to find that warm place between her thighs and rub her clit, spreading the moisture. God, it felt so good. So naughty, doing this out in the open.

"Clay . . ." Her voice was breathy. Growing more excited.

"Let's get these pants out of the way so I can make you feel really good, baby." Grabbing the waistband, he shucked them down along with her panties, leaving them at her calves. Then he spun her to face the barn. "Hands on the wall, spread your feet out more."

"I've never done anything like this before," she breathed. "Outside, I mean." But she assumed the position eagerly.

"That's part of what makes it so fun." Smoothing his palms over her hips and the round globes of her ass. "Spread a little more. That's my baby. Tell me what you want."

"I—I want you to fuck me." She poked her ass back, inviting him.

"How do you want it? Tell me." With his right hand, he skimmed under the curve of her ass. Took two fingers and parted her folds, and rubbed the slit. Then worked inside to fuck her channel, drive her crazy.

"H-hard and fast. Fuck me like you mean it!"

He rumbled in approval. Behind her, she heard him unzip his jeans, felt his motions as he freed his dripping cock. Then he brought the head to her entrance and began to push into her heat.

"Shit, yes. You're so hot and tight, baby. Brace yourself, because I'm gonna give you a good, hard ride."

"Do it."

"Shit, you're so pretty, I could almost come just from this, the sight of my woman spread for me. Wet and ready for my cock. You're mine."

"Yours! Oh, yes . . . all the way, I need you in me!"

He thrust to the hilt and stilled for a few seconds, gripping her waist. He stayed that way as if it took all his willpower not to succumb to fucking her too hard and getting off too soon.

Then he began to take her in unhurried but powerful strokes. The slap of their slick skin drove her crazy, and her channel clasping, squeezing his rod, sent her lover to the edge in minutes.

"I'm not going to last," he warned her.

"I don't care! Fuck me hard!"

He increased the tempo some, putting even more strength behind the strokes. Enough to send them both into ecstasy, but not enough to hurt her.

Her orgasm hit suddenly and she cried out, undulating on his cock, milking him. Her lover's release was explosive and he came endlessly, hard and deep. Just like she'd wanted.

All too soon they were spent and he pulled out carefully, placing a gentle kiss between her shoulder blades. "Thank you, baby. You were incredible."

"So were you." Turning, she gave him a blazing kiss. When he pulled back, she couldn't help but stare, awed by his raw masculinity. His possessiveness.

The truth hit her hard—she'd fallen in love with him. No question. This man who made her feel special, who'd claimed her heart and soul.

She could only pray his feelings were the same.

* * *

The call came in at five thirty a.m. the next morning.

Clay blinked sleepily and groaned, rolling over to snatch his cell phone from the nightstand before the ringing woke up Melissa. Calls this early never boded well.

When he saw that the incoming call was from Six-Pack, however, he felt a thrill go through him. He hoped . . . "Hello?"

"I'm glad you answered," his captain said. "Julian and Eve are *both* out with the flu and we're seriously shorthanded. Sorry to spring this on you, but you think you can start today instead of Monday?"

Excitement coursed through him and he bolted upright in bed. "Are you kidding? You bet I can! Sorry they're sick and all, but damn, I'm *so* ready to get back to work."

Howard chuckled. "I figured you wouldn't mind too much. See you soon."

"Can't wait. I mean that."

After saying good-bye, he ended the call and sat grinning from ear to ear. This was the day! Hot damn!

"Why are you practically vibrating in bed at oh-God-thirty in the morning, looking like you've just won the lottery?" Melissa grumbled from beside him.

Setting down the phone, he pounced on her, kissing her senseless. Then, arms braced on the pillow on either side of her head, he said, "That was Howard. He needs me to start today!"

She blinked as it took a few seconds for his words to register. Then she smiled and cupped his cheeks. "I'm so glad. This is the day you've been waiting for. Why the change from Monday?"

"Julian and Eve have the flu. Apparently something is going around."

"Well, I'm sorry about that, but glad for you."

"Me, too."

"When do you have to be there?"

"Seven. So, I've got an hour and a half to get ready and get to the station." He paused, giving her a heated look, and ground his morning wood into her thigh. "Just enough time."

"You're insatiable," she said, rolling her eyes. But she held him close and didn't protest at all as he took a series of kisses to the next level.

And way beyond.

Half an hour later, sweaty and sated, he pulled his woman from the bed and into the shower. Morning sex, a beautiful woman of his own, and his job back. His life couldn't be more complete.

He was happy, he realized. Not simply content, but totally over the moon, for the first time.

I'm falling for her. No, I've fallen. It's much too late to guard my heart now, even if I wanted to. Which I don't.

Is this love?

Maybe. He'd never said those three little words to

a woman before, and his mother didn't count. Well, she counted, just not in the same way.

As they got dressed, he contemplated how to discuss his new feelings with her. When and where. A romantic, candlelit dinner? Or while they were out hiking or something, on a picnic? Crap, he had no idea. Maybe he should ask his mom for advice, or his friends, but he wasn't so sure.

All too soon, they were in his car and headed for the police station. He pulled up in front of the building.

"I guess I should've taken you home to get your car," he said. "I was going to pick you up after you got off work, and now I'll be on shift for twenty-four hours."

"It's not a problem," she assured him, giving him a peck on the lips. "I'll get one of the guys to take me home."

"If you're sure . . ."

"I am." Her green gaze lit him from the inside out. "Have a great first day back, and text me when you can."

"I'll do that. You have a good day, too, sweetheart."

Reluctantly, he watched her go, wishing they didn't have to be separated by even a few hours. *You've got it bad.*

Once she'd waved and then disappeared into the building, he put the car in gear and continued on his way. When he got to the street leading to Station Five, he turned right. Just as he did, he noted a dark SUV making a left behind him, heading in the other direction.

A chill went through him. *Fucking paranoid, that's what you are.* But what if he wasn't? Who could be following them? Her uncle? If Melissa wasn't exaggerating, and he didn't think she was, James Ryan was quite the unsavory character—just like his nephew, who'd been sent back to prison after the wreck.

If Ryan was following them, he was being pretty overt about it. That in and of itself was troubling. If he *wanted* them to notice, that meant he was trying to freak them out on purpose. He was playing cat and mouse—to what end, Clay couldn't imagine. But whatever the end game, it couldn't be good.

After parking in the station's lot, he shot a quick text to Melissa: *Saw that SUV again. Think it's the same, but not sure. Turned off just as I got close to the station. WTF??*

He got a quick answer: *IDK. B careful.*

U 2. Then he added a heart emoji and sent. He grinned as he got one in return.

The big doors to all the bays were open as he approached, which was typical. The quint, engine, truck, and ambulance all sat in their spots, red and sparkling. He felt a pang of gratitude to be back, ready to start the rest of his life.

What wasn't typical was the absence of any of the guys hanging out in the bay. It was just before shift change, and there should be lots of activity. C-shift should be leaving, Clay's A-shift arriving, lots of banter all around. There was nobody. Weird.

He crossed the bay to the door that led inside the station proper, and halted in his tracks when he saw the words on the glass door. They were backward, facing inside for those who were leaving to enter the bay, but he knew what they said.

Everybody Goes Home.

He shuddered, thinking of the last time he'd read those words, before he and Julian climbed into the ambulance. Before that fateful ride to the call they'd never made it to. For a couple of seconds, he heard Julian call out. Saw the grill of a truck barreling toward his side.

He almost hadn't made it home. But he *had* survived, and he was ready to reclaim his place. That made him proud, and he reached for the handle, pulling the door open.

As he entered the short hallway leading to the kitchen, he didn't hear any voices. Inside, it was silent as a tomb. Not typical at all. He barely had time to process what was going on as he entered the kitchen and a collective shout nearly deafened him.

"Surprise!"

Bodies popped up from behind the kitchen counters and the tables, chairs, and the nearby sofa. He stared in awe as he realized every single firefighter who worked at Station Five—from all three shifts—was there. Every single person was present, and they were all suddenly surrounding him, slapping him on the back and giving him manly hugs.

"Shit, you guys!" he exclaimed. "You're going to make me bawl, and then I'll never hear the end of it!" This earned a laugh from the eager crowd.

"Go ahead," Six-Pack said, grinning as he stepped forward. "You've earned it, and nobody will say a word."

With that, the big captain pulled him into a bear hug that nearly squashed his lungs. Clay didn't mind one bit. As they broke apart, Clay marveled at the turnout, which was bigger than he'd expected. There were dispatchers from the department present, and a couple of the secretaries as well. Battalion Chief Sean Tanner hurried forward, giving him the same treatment as Six-Pack, as Sean's wife, Eve, stood by smiling.

Even Chief Ben Paxton, Six-Pack's father, was there.

Tears stung his eyes at the outpouring of love from his entire department. He barely kept from losing it as he turned to Howard and smiled.

"There never was any case of the flu, I take it," he said, gesturing to Eve and Julian, who were dressed for their shifts and looking healthy as could be.

"Nope. We wanted to surprise you, and the consensus was that you might expect something if we stuck with having you start on Monday. This way, you probably wouldn't expect a thing." He looked awfully proud of himself.

"I don't know if I would've expected anything this big. But you're right, I was damned surprised!"

His friends were pleased that they'd gotten one over on him. Soon, they were all digging into the huge, hot breakfast spread laid out on the counters and table. Everyone had brought some sort of home-made covered dish, and there was plenty of coffee and juice, too. Belatedly, he noted the balloons and the banner that declared, *Welcome Home, Clay!*

This place *was* home. Always would be. The morning couldn't have been any more perfect.

He visited with everyone he could, thanking every person he saw. Eventually, the party wound down and people started to leave, some of them saying they'd see him on Saturday for Howard's cookout, where they'd do some real celebrating. As the last of the guests left and only his team remained behind, Clay thought about texting Melissa and telling her about his surprise party, but decided to wait. A text message couldn't do justice to how great this had made him feel.

"It's really awesome to have you back," Eve said, hugging him around one shoulder. "We've missed the hell out of you."

"I'm getting that idea. Thank you all for this. I mean that from the bottom of my heart."

Zack winked at him. "Hey, we had to take measures to bring you in. You've been out long enough, you slacker."

He laughed, and it felt good.

"Seriously," Jamie put in. "Everything's all healed? No complications?"

Clay studied their new guy. He was a nice kid, and Clay liked him. "The knee twinges now and then, but my doctor cleared me for work. It'll hold, and I'm good to go."

"That's great, man. I'm happy for you."

"Thanks." They did a knuckle bump, and then Clay noticed something about Jamie's face. "Where'd you get those bruises?"

The younger man ducked his head. "Oh, I just got into a little skirmish in downtown Nashville the other night. No big."

"Oh. Well, hope the other dude got the worst of it."

"I wish. I'm not much of a fighter. I'm made to rescue people, not hurt them." Jamie looked uncomfortable with the direction their talk had taken. "I'm going to help clean up the kitchen."

As he hurried away, Clay noted the look of concern on Zack's face while he watched Jamie go. Clay moved closer to Zack and lowered his voice. "What do you make of that?"

"I don't know." Zack sighed. "This isn't the first time he's come in with bruises in the past few months, and he always has a ready excuse. I won't lie, we're worried about him."

"Is he missing work?"

"No. He's always on time, and seems really glad to be here. He's an asset to the team."

"You think someone's beating him?" Clay asked quietly.

Zack nodded slowly. "Yeah, I do. Whatever is going on, he's not ready to talk about it."

Shit. This was *so* not good. "Does he still live with his parents?"

"No, and that was my first thought, too—maybe a dad with quick fists. But his folks live in Florida. He says he lives alone, but I'm not so sure."

From across the room, Clay noted how Jamie moved around with some stiffness, favoring his side from time to time. "I don't think the bruises are just on his face, Zack."

"I agree." His gaze darkened. "And if we're right about this, his life could depend on whether he opens up and accepts help."

"We'll just have to do all we can to make sure he knows we're here for him. Every one of us has contacts we can utilize if he's got an abuser."

"Yeah. I hope we can get him to talk."

Jamie glanced over at them with a frown, and Clay realized he was probably getting suspicious with them standing there in serious conversation while looking over at him. Quickly, Zack changed the subject.

"So, how about those Titans? Think we're headed for the Super Bowl this year?"

Clay grabbed on to the subject, and they passed the time arguing about football as they cleaned up the rest of the party stuff. His happiness at returning was tempered by the thought of whatever hell Jamie was going through. But his mood picked up as the day went on, and they finally got a call.

They were summoned to a local elementary school, where a kid had gotten his head stuck between the bars of an iron fence. He snorted, amused. Kids found all sorts of predicaments to get themselves into.

"Want me to drive?" Julian offered, jingling the keys to the ambulance. They probably wouldn't need to rush the kid to the hospital, but taking the vehicle was a precaution.

Clay shook his head. "No, I'll drive. Best to get that elephant out of the room right away, don't you think?"

Julian's smile split his face. "That's my boy." Then he tossed Clay the keys.

Sliding behind the wheel had never felt so right. "Let's do this."

All the way to their call, Clay was more cautious and alert than ever and watched the traffic like a hawk. He was surprised he wasn't more freaked out to be behind the wheel of the ambulance again, but glad.

This, as far as he was concerned, was his last hurdle, and he'd cleared it. They got to the school in one piece.

And he didn't spot a single dark SUV following them along the way.

7

Melissa was hard at some paperwork when Captain Austin Rainey stuck his head in the door.

"Ryan," he said in greeting, then stepped inside. His expression was grim. "You got a minute?"

"Sure, Cap." Rising, she tried to quell the icy clench in her gut. She couldn't think of a thing she'd done wrong, but nasty surprises could come from all sides. "What can I do for you?"

Moving inside, he closed the door, leaving just the two of them. "I've been made aware of a situation, and it has to be handled with the utmost discretion." He paused, the silence weighty. "One of our officers is missing, and I need for you to dig around, find out anything you can as to his whereabouts."

Her heart skipped a beat and she stood, walking over to the captain. "Missing? Oh, no. Who is it?"

"Officer Ron Nelson. He's forty-five, been in the department over twenty years. You know him?"

"No, but I know who he is." She thought for a few seconds. "The last time I saw him was after he answered the robbery call at the gas station. We spoke briefly, but that was it. When was he last on shift?"

Austin raked a hand through his hair. "He worked the day before yesterday, then left around five thirty p.m. He called his wife from his cell to say he was picking up Chinese on the way home, but he never arrived at his house."

Melissa pulled out her notebook. "Does she know where he stopped?"

"A place called New Hong Kong over on Barrett Street. He used his credit card, so the restaurant had no trouble confirming that he picked up his order."

"Just because his credit card was used doesn't mean he's the one who picked up the order," she mused.

"True. But we have an eyewitness who claims it was, in fact, Nelson who picked up his food, and he was still in uniform. The kid described him to a T, and we've been able to pull some security footage from the restaurant as well."

"And the trail goes cold from there," she guessed.

"You got it."

"Okay, I'll review the footage and then go talk to

the people at the restaurant. Maybe someone knows something they don't realize they know."

"That's what you get paid the big bucks for," he said. But his teasing was halfhearted.

Anyone going missing was serious business, and they would act swiftly to try to find Nelson. But in recent news, with officers being persecuted, shot, and murdered on a regular basis, for one of their own to disappear without a trace was especially alarming.

"I'll do my best to find him, Cap."

"I know you will. The video from the restaurant is in room three. I'll meet you there." After clapping her on the shoulder, he turned and walked out.

Quickly, she grabbed a pen, her purse, and her cell phone, and hurried after him. She'd need to go into the field, and didn't have her car. She'd have to check out an unmarked squad, which she hated doing, but it couldn't be helped.

In the small room that was set up with computers and the video she needed to see, she took a seat next to Austin. With them was a tech man, Sam, and another officer, Mac Reed, a good friend of Nelson's.

Sam pulled up the video feed and hit the play button. Instantly, she saw a uniformed officer who was obviously Ron Nelson walk into the restaurant and approach the counter. Nelson hesitated, looking behind him, then proceeded on. The video was mundane and didn't reveal much. It did show the kid who'd identified the officer, but nothing else. Except . . .

"Play it again," she said. They did, and she sat up straight, pointing at the screen. "Pause it. Now go back and play that part again."

"What are we looking at?" Sam asked.

"That hesitation," the captain said, narrowing his eyes. "Ron paused and looked behind him. Is he frowning?"

"Can't tell, but look how he briefly rests a hand on his weapon." She pointed. "He was bothered by something. Do we have a video of outside, when he's coming and going?"

Sam confirmed. "We do, but it's sort of dark and not good quality. It does show him, though."

"Let's see it."

They watched, and at first, it appeared to show little if anything. Nelson arrived, stayed a couple of minutes, just long enough to pay for his order, then left with the food in his hands. But something, some shadow, seemed to move in the background.

"What is that?" she asked, pointing.

Sam replayed the video, but it was still hard to tell. Then he did a screen capture of the object and blew it up. When he finally brought the image up enough where it could be seen, Melissa's blood ran cold.

"It's the front end of a dark SUV," she said softly. "Just like the one that's been following me."

"What?" Rainey asked sharply, staring at her. "What the fuck?"

"A dark SUV followed me and Clay yesterday, then

trailed him to work this morning. I wasn't sure before, but I'm pretty positive now that we weren't being paranoid." The icy ball in her gut grew into a glacier.

"What reason would anyone have to follow you? Or Ron, for that matter?" Austin's eyes bored into hers.

"Why it would follow Ron, I couldn't say. But I suspect if it's following me, then my uncle is involved somehow."

The captain nodded. "I remember what you told me about him. We can't touch him—that's the government's area unless he commits a crime in town that we can arrest him for. Has he threatened you?"

"No, and that's the thing. He's been strangely silent since I returned to Sugarland, and my uncle is not the quiet type. I'm sure he knows I'm here. Any silence from his end can only be construed as suspicious at best, dangerous at worst."

"You think he'll make a move soon." It wasn't a question.

"I'm really afraid he may have already." Chewing on her lower lip, she stared at the video screen.

"All right." Austin leaned forward. "Let's assume he or someone he hired has been following you and Clay. Then let's assume he followed Ron, and possibly worse. To what end would he hurt an officer you barely know?"

"My uncle knows me well enough to understand

that it would hurt me for someone to target any officer who's been close to me. If he's been following me for long, he knows Ron and I worked a call together and saw us talking. It would be enough of a warning to me if he grabbed Ron."

"What kind of warning?"

"That he can get to me or any of my colleagues anytime he wants. Sadly, that's true."

They fell silent for a few moments, and then Melissa pushed to her feet. "I'll get going with those interviews and do some poking around. Best case, we'll find him shaken but unharmed."

Nobody had to voice the worst case.

"In light of this discussion, I want you to take one of your team with you. Take Shane, he's around here somewhere."

"But Cap—"

"That wasn't a discussion." His clipped tone and stiff body language shut her trap real quick.

"Yes, sir."

"Good. Two heads are better than one, as they say. It's not just for your protection."

"You're right, of course. I'll go find Shane."

"Let me know when you find something."

When, not if. With a nod, she walked out and went in search of her wayward lead detective. It didn't escape Melissa's notice that Austin was sending her out with his very best homicide detective. She shivered inside at the knowledge of what that meant—

after nearly forty-eight hours without a word from Ron following a normal stop to pick up food after work? The poor man was probably dead.

Still, he could be injured somewhere, lying around waiting for help. She clung to that as she found Shane in the break room sucking down coffee like it held the secret to everlasting life. They were alone, so she spoke in a low tone as she reached him.

"Ron Nelson from patrol is missing. Austin wants us on it."

Shane's eyes widened and he tossed his paper cup. "No shit? Give me the rundown."

She did, leaving nothing out, and he whistled quietly. "I want to see the videos before we head out."

"I figured you would. We'll let you watch and then go check out an unmarked."

"Fuck that, we'll take my truck. Nothing ever really gets the stench of piss and vomit out of the backseat."

"Gross. That's one of the reasons I don't miss patrol."

"Same here."

She watched the video with Shane, who hummed thoughtfully before agreeing that the SUV was definitely suspicious and gave them a new angle to follow.

"We'll canvass some of the nearby businesses, see if they have a video showing the parking lot of the Chinese place and if they'll release it."

"That's a big if. Many businesses won't let go of their vids without a court order."

"I've never been able to understand that." He shook his head as they walked out together. "Why do some people resist helping when they have evidence that could solve a crime or even save a life?"

"Because they don't want to get involved, or they hate cops. Any number of reasons. It's damned frustrating."

He made a noise of agreement. "Maybe luck will be on our side."

It wasn't.

The employees at New Hong Kong had nothing to add to the witness's statement, nor had any of them seen the alleged SUV in question. After a bit more probing, they left and hit the surrounding businesses. Only one had a viable feed of the parking lot of that night, but the manager wouldn't let them see it, much less release it, without the okay from corporate.

"Back to square one," Shane muttered in disgust. "The little fucker. What would it have hurt to let us at least look?"

"Cop hater," she said. "He sneered at you when you weren't looking. I barely caught him. That vid has probably hit the trash can as we speak."

"Yeah. Son of a bitch." He climbed behind the wheel and slammed the door. "I've got a bad feeling about Ron."

"Me, too." She checked her phone. "Just got a text from Austin—Ron's wife says she checked their on-line account with their cell phone service provider, and there's been no activity on Ron's phone. Not good."

"Sure isn't. They can't pinpoint a location?"

"No. It's either dead or turned off, and he didn't have a locater app installed on it."

Looking as disheartened as she felt, Shane started the truck. "Let's drive his route home, see if we can find anything."

"Good idea. I can't believe nobody's done that yet," she said.

"I'm sure his wife did, plus Mac and some of the other patrol officers, but it won't hurt to give the area a fresh eye."

They drove out I-49, carefully scanning the gullies and forest along the side of the road for any breaks. Any flash of color among the green and brown. Ron's car, they'd been told, was a recent-model blue Taurus, and the dark shade of the paint job might be hard to spot among the shadows of the gullies.

They were disappointed not to find anything. No crushed foliage, no skid marks or debris. Nothing to indicate a wreck had taken place—at least not on Ron's normal route home.

"Let's take that side road we passed a couple of miles back," she suggested. "There aren't many places to pull off the road on this winding stretch, and if he felt ill or had car trouble, he might've turned off there."

It was a stretch, but they had nothing else.

The road was built on an incline, bordered by a fence on one side. She was glad they'd brought Shane's truck to navigate the terrain. There wasn't much to see, until she spotted something off to her right.

"Stop!" Immediately he hit the brakes. "Look, over there."

His eyes followed where she was pointing, to a break in the fence. It was nearly concealed by weeds, but the area, including the plants, had clearly been crushed.

"Good eye," he said, putting the truck in park. "Let's see what we've got."

What they had was a spot where a vehicle of some type had definitely gone through the fence. The break was wide enough for a car, and the tire tread marks in the dirt gave proof.

"No car, though." He frowned. "Where could it be, assuming it was Ron's?"

"Well, if he was fleeing someone, or wanted to make a stand and confront his pursuer, I'm guessing he pulled off here. But he lost control and went through the fence. He gets out, and the confrontation goes bad. He's subdued and the suspect takes him."

"And comes back for his car later. Damn, Ron could be anywhere."

"Exactly."

They continued their search, moving farther off the road. Melissa wasn't thinking they'd find much else—until she spotted a few dark droplets on some leaves about twenty yards from the broken fence.

"Shane, I got something."

He came to take a look. "Dried blood? We need to get the crime scene techs in here to process this. Might not be the scene we're looking for, but something occurred here and we need to find out what."

She agreed. Shane made the call, and an hour later they were up to their elbows in cops and crime scene personnel. The captain showed up, too, and took in the area for himself. Pictures were snapped. Lots of samples of the soil, leaves, and blood were taken, and several hours later, she and Shane were among the last to depart.

"Jesus, I'm tired," he complained. "Just standing around is worse than chasing a suspect on foot for twenty blocks."

"True that."

She was relieved when they climbed into his truck to leave. After some maneuvering, he managed to turn the vehicle around and get them onto the highway again. As he pointed the truck toward town, they were each lost in their own thoughts. She thought of the possible crime scene, and couldn't fathom what Ron's wife was going through.

If it were Clay who was missing and probably dead, she'd lose her mind. That didn't even bear thinking about.

"Hey, check out this van on our six."

Glancing behind them, she saw a white utility van closing the distance at a rapid pace. The driver was going much too fast on these roads.

"Shit, he's not going to slow down," Shane growled, speeding up.

But the van had caught up to them, and Melissa barely had time to brace herself before the driver slammed into them from behind.

"Goddammit! That prick!" Shane yelled. His truck fishtailed wildly before he gained control. "What the fuck is he doing?"

"Here he comes again!"

Fear coursed through her like lightning and she yelled out as the van hit them again. Shane fought the steering wheel, trying to correct the truck's forward motion. But the effort was useless. The heavy vehicle skidded, hit the gravel on the shoulder . . .

And plunged over the side of the steep embankment.

Melissa shrieked and Shane cursed as the truck shot down the incline, bouncing over rocks, the jolts hard enough to rattle their bones. She felt a sharp pain in her mouth and warmth flooded her tongue. The trees were approaching at frightening speed.

And then the truck began to slide sideways, tilting. They were along for the ride as it rolled in a terrible crunch of metal, and the world flipped once. Twice. Her head smacked against the window and she flailed, attempting to shield herself from more damage.

The truck landed upright with a hard thud, slid a few more feet, then came to rest against a tree on Shane's side.

"Oh my God," she gasped, reaching a shaking hand to the throbbing spot on her head. "Are you all right?"

Silence. Ominous, absolute quiet.

"Shane?" Dreading what she would see, she looked over at her friend.

The other detective was utterly still and pale, eyes closed. Blood streamed from under his sable hair and down the side of his face, and his head was tilted slightly to the side, resting against the window.

"No," she whispered. "Don't be dead. Please, please, be okay."

Hand trembling, she reached out and pressed two fingers to his neck. At first she found nothing, and began to panic. But finally she located his pulse, which seemed to be steady and strong.

"Thank God."

Now to get help. Finding a cell phone was the first order of business. She patted her front pants pocket to find hers still stuck there, and fished it out. The device appeared undamaged. But when she unlocked the screen and tried to make a call, there was no service.

"Dammit!"

The reception in the gulley was shit. She'd have to climb to higher ground to get a signal. It took her several tries to get her door open, and she had to shove so hard she almost spilled onto the ground when it gave. Looking worriedly back at Shane, she checked his breathing one more time to find his chest rising and falling in slow rhythm. Then she stumbled from the truck and started the arduous climb to the top.

As steep as it had looked going down, it was worse going up. Halfway there, her legs were shaking and rubbery. Stopping, she checked her phone for service. When she saw the little bars across the top indicating a connection, she could've wept with relief. Quickly, she placed the call.

"Nine-one-one, what is your emergency?" the dispatcher intoned.

"This is Detective Melissa Ryan, Sugarland PD," she rasped. "My colleague and I, Detective Shane Ford, have just been run off the road. His truck rolled and is lying in a gulley off I-49. We need police and an ambulance, and please hurry!"

"Detective Ryan, can you give me an idea of your location?"

Melissa described the spot as best as she could, and the dispatcher affirmed that help was coming and to stay on the line. "I'm going to continue on to the top so I can see the road and wave them down. Please hurry, Detective Ford is bleeding and unconscious."

Another thought struck her—what if the truck caught fire and blew up? *Oh, God. Should I go back and get him out?*

"Okay, hang tight, Detective. Help is on the way."

"What if the truck catches on fire? I need to go back and get him out."

"Do you see any smoke?" the other woman asked.

Looking down at the vehicle, she peered closely and relaxed only marginally. "No, I don't. But I hate not being able to help him."

"You *are* helping him, okay? Continue to the top and flag down the first responders so they don't miss you. If they pass you by, it will cause a delay getting assistance to Detective Ford. Can you do that?"

The dispatcher's voice was calm, and her reasoning broke through Melissa's rising panic. "Yes, I can do that. I'm going now."

She absolutely hated leaving Shane. The most helpless feeling in the world was continuing on knowing he was injured and bleeding in the cab of his truck. But the dispatcher was right—the most pressing concern was making sure their help actually found them.

At the top, she bent over panting with exertion, hands on her knees. Little black spots danced before her eyes, but she wasn't going to pass out now. Forcing herself to calm down, she took slow breaths until the dizziness and black spots faded.

The noise of a car on the road caught her attention. Ignoring the pain making itself known in her battered body, she waved frantically as a squad car rounded the bend. The officer pulled off onto the shoulder and she saw the car held two occupants in the front—the uniformed officer named Jenk, and Austin Rainey. He must've just gotten back to the station after investigating the potential crime scene and had been nearby when she placed the call for help.

"Thank God," she said on a sob as they approached. Austin wrapped her in a quick hug and she leaned into his strength for a moment. Then she pulled away and pointed into the gulley. "Shane's down there and he's hurt."

Both men cursed. The captain gently took her arms in his big hands and said, "Wait here for the ambulance, all right? We'll go down to Shane."

She nodded tearfully. "Okay. I wanted so much to stay with him. Please tell him."

"We will," he assured her with a soft smile.

Then he and Jenk were hurrying down the incline, skidding, shoes kicking up rocks and dust in their haste. From her vantage point she could see Jenk walk around to the driver's side, but shake his head. The tree was in the way. Austin crawled in through the open passenger's door to get to the other detective, and then Melissa couldn't see much through the truck's tinted and cracked windows. Shane had someone with him now, and that was what mattered.

When she heard the sirens, the deep horn of the fire engine, her hand went over her mouth. Emotion crashed through her, wild and raw, as she spotted the ambulance coming round the bend, the engine behind it, lights and sirens blaring.

And she burst into tears.

So far, it had been a busy first day back at the station.

Not that Clay was complaining—far from it. He relished being busy, having a purpose again. He chuckled to himself, thinking of the eight-year-old who had his head stuck in the fence earlier. The kid hadn't cried or anything as he waited for the firefighters to dismantle the iron bars so they could free him, but he'd been plenty embarrassed.

They'd given him some Sugarland Fire Department logo stickers and a stuffed Sparky the Fire Dog to brighten his day. But when Clay's team had left, the boy's playground friends had been chanting, "Way to go, Iron Man!"

The poor little guy would probably be stuck with that moniker for the rest of his public school days.

Clay had just bitten into a chocolate chip cookie when three loud tones sounded over the intercom system, announcing an incoming call. This time it was a truck that had gone off the road out on I-49, and there was an occupant trapped inside.

Nothing amusing whatsoever about this one. The drive down that stretch of highway was a gorgeous one—but it was also extremely treacherous. Clay shoved the rest of the cookie in his mouth and jogged for the bay, then jumped into his boots and pulled on his turnouts. The rest of his team followed suit, and they were roaring down the street in seconds.

Julian drove the ambulance this time, and Clay sat in the passenger's seat nearly vibrating with adrenaline. He lived for this, helping people. And now, having been a victim of a near-tragic accident himself, he had a whole new level of empathy for the people who relied on him to rescue them.

Several minutes later, Julian rounded a bend in the highway and his eyes widened. "Say, isn't that your new girlfriend?"

"Holy shit!" he exclaimed. "What the hell?"

As Julian pulled over and parked behind the squad car, Clay saw that Melissa's shirt was torn and a trickle of blood was running down the side of her pale face. Her eyes were trained frantically on the arriving assistance, and her hand went over her mouth. She looked like she was barely holding on to her sanity.

He was out of the ambulance in a split second. "Melissa!"

She launched herself into his arms and fell apart, sobbing into his shoulder. He held her close, patting her hair, crooning in her ear that he had her and wasn't letting go. Who the hell had done this to his girl? Rage gripped him and he wanted to kill someone for this. But he kept his control for her sake, just barely.

"What happened, baby?" he whispered into her hair.

"A van ran us off the road," she said with a hiccup. She still clung to him like a burr.

Son of a bitch! "Do you know who it was?"

"No. It happened so fast. He came out of nowhere and started hitting us from behind."

"The driver did this on purpose?" he asked with tightly veiled anger.

"Yes. I'll bet anything my uncle's behind this, and now Shane's hurt."

Shit, shit.

His team rushed past, except for Six-Pack, who stopped to nod at Clay. "Tend to Melissa. You can assist us once you decide she's okay."

"You got it."

The captain gave Melissa an encouraging smile, then hurried to help his team extract Shane from the truck. Clay was grateful that he'd assigned Melissa's care to him. She was a victim as well, and he'd use his training to help her the same as he would anyone else.

"Come sit in the back of the ambulance so I can check you out," he said, guiding her carefully toward the vehicle.

"I'm fine," she tried to protest. But he was having none of it.

"Who's the paramedic here? Hmm? Go with me on this one."

He was glad she offered no further resistance. Though she was shaky on her feet, she made it well enough with him holding on to her arm, and he sat her in the back. Quickly he retrieved some cleansing wipes and bandages, a blood pressure cuff, and a stethoscope.

"Where does it hurt, sweetheart?"

"All over," she mumbled.

"Anywhere in particular?" He took a small light and shined it into each eye. She was a bit shocky, maybe slightly concussed.

"Smacked my head, but I don't think it's too bad. Just a cut."

He examined the area just under her hairline and agreed. "It's a small cut and probably doesn't need stitches. I'm going to clean it, then close it with a butterfly bandage. Okay, baby?"

She nodded, looking tired and wilting more every minute. He longed to take her home, lay her down, and hold her for the rest of the evening, and it hurt him that he couldn't. He was on shift until seven in the morning. His mind worked on the problem of who was going to care for her until he got off work.

And then he knew. He'd spring that news on her later.

Soon he had her wound dressed and had checked her vitals. Other than being a bit battered, she would be all right, and his gratitude knew no bounds.

Someone had tried to kill his love. And Shane, too. Was it James Ryan? Would he try again? When, and how would he come at her?

He wanted to help his team, but suddenly he didn't want to leave her sitting there alone and vulnerable. Just then, a uniformed officer and a tall, well-built auburn-haired man in a suit appeared at the top of the incline and made their way over to where he was tending Melissa.

"Austin Rainey," the man in the suit said to him pleasantly, extending his hand. "I'm a captain at the police department, and one of Detective Ryan's superiors. How is she?"

Rainey had an easy manner, carried himself straight. There was an intelligence and confidence about the man that drew Clay. He liked the captain instantly.

"She'll be fine, but we're still going to take her in to the ER to get checked out."

"I think that's for the best." The captain addressed his detective in a tone that brooked no argument. "When you're done at the hospital, you're off today and tomorrow. That takes us into the weekend, so I don't technically want to see you at work until Monday."

"But—"

"That's an order, Detective."

She slumped. "Yes, sir."

Austin looked to Clay. "I assume she'll be in good hands?"

The man was perceptive. "Very much so, sir."

"Good."

"How's Shane?" Clay asked.

The captain's expression darkened. "I'm not sure. He was coming around when your team arrived. They're bringing him up now."

Just as Rainey spoke those words, his teammates appeared at the top, carrying Shane strapped to a backboard. His neck was in a brace, his face bloodied, eyes open. That he was conscious was a very good sign, but that didn't mean the detective was out of the woods.

Melissa slid from the back of the ambulance to make way for her friend. Clay pulled the gurney out of the back to get it ready, and his team placed the backboard onto it. Shane was awake, but appeared dazed. Zack stepped up to give Clay the rundown.

"BP is good, no broken bones that we could detect, and there doesn't appear to be any internal injuries. His head took a hard whack, though, and he's definitely got a concussion."

Clay nodded, then looked down at the detective. "Shane? It's Clay Montana. Can you hear me?"

Slowly, Shane's cloudy gaze found his. "Yeah," he croaked. "Fuck . . ."

Clay smiled. "You can respond, and as an added bonus, you've retained your ability to curse. All good signs." His easy bedside manner made his patient's lips curve up in a half smile. It was part of how firefighters made people feel a little better and at ease after the shock of being hurt.

Quickly, they got Shane loaded into the back of the ambulance, and then Clay helped Melissa inside. She took the seat opposite Clay, across the gurney that was holding Shane. Zack slammed the doors, shutting them inside. Once Julian climbed back into the driver's seat, they were on their way.

With an effort, Clay concentrated on tending to Shane, and sending his love an encouraging smile now and then. *Focus on healing, comforting. That's what you do.*

But the pep talk was no use.

If Clay found out who'd done this, he was one dead motherfucker.

8

Clay had developed a hatred of hospitals.

That was unfortunate, considering his team ended up there on just about every single shift. Oh, he had a healthy respect for the doctors and nurses who put people such as himself back together, even when there was seemingly no hope. It was the place itself, the white walls, the sounds and smells, that he loathed.

They brought back dark memories of endless pain and suffering. Long days and nights of wishing he'd died upon impact.

He didn't feel that way now, was grateful he'd survived. But it had been an agonizing road. The journey made him empathize even more with the victims he sought to assist.

The ER was ordered chaos, as usual, when they brought Melissa and Shane inside. His team hung around for a bit, letting him make sure his lady was taken care of before they headed back to the station.

"It's fine, as long as we don't get another call," Six-Pack told him.

"Thanks, Cap."

"Hey, if it was my Kat, I'd be here, too."

Their unwavering support never failed to humble him. Following through on the decision he'd made earlier, he placed a call and hoped Melissa wouldn't be too annoyed with him. But there was no way he was leaving her alone for the rest of his shift, so she could just get over it.

Afterward, with things settled, he wandered back to the room where they were finishing up with her. As soon as he saw her, his heart melted. The tough cop had been replaced by his exhausted baby. She looked so small and forlorn sitting there on the bed.

"Hey, baby." He smiled and went to her, standing between her legs to gather her close. "Any word on Shane?"

"Daisy and Drew are here, and they came by to see me. Just as your team thought, he's got a concussion, but no broken bones or internal injuries. They said the doctor's going to send him home, but they have to watch him closely overnight."

"That's great news."

"The best. For a few seconds after we stopped rolling, and he wouldn't answer me . . ." She couldn't go on, and her lips trembled.

"I know, sweetheart." He cupped her chin, gazing into her watery green eyes. "But he's going to be fine, and so are you."

He held her for a few more minutes, until the nurse came by with her release papers. As soon as she was free to go, she sighed.

"I guess I'll call the station and get a ride home."

"No, you absolutely won't," he told her. "I've got you covered."

"How?" She frowned. "You've got to go back to work."

"Because you've got me, precious girl, that's how," a new voice said.

Melissa blinked past him and Clay grinned, knowing the cavalry had come to the rescue.

"Mrs. Montana?"

"Charlene," his mother corrected her. "Ready to go? Because you're coming home with me until my son gets off work."

"Oh, no, I couldn't possible impose on you like that!"

"Impose? Sweetie, you're practically family now, and family takes care of their own." Charlene pushed Clay out of the way and gave the other woman a motherly hug. Melissa sank into the embrace, apparently soaking up the attention. Clay realized how starved she must be for a mother's attention, and his heart clenched.

Thank God for Mom. She's the greatest ever.

"I suppose I'm ready, then," Melissa said. "If you're sure."

"Let's go, sweet girl. Let me take care of you, and you'll feel better in the morning."

Clay walked them out and kissed them both goodbye. "I'll see you both in the morning," he told Melissa. Then to his mom, "Thanks for this."

"No thanks needed," she said, waving him off. "I always wanted a daughter to mother, now I have one."

He flushed some at that, since he and Melissa hadn't had *The Discussion* yet about making things permanent. But he was quickly coming to realize that he and his lady were naturally progressing toward that status as a couple. Already had, if the truth were known.

His mother and Melissa left together, and Clay made a mental note to make sure they were on the same page with where they were going as a couple. Part of him was afraid she'd say she wanted to wait, not get too serious, but he didn't think that was the case.

Putting all of that from his mind for the time being, he walked over to his team. "Ready when you guys are."

"Helluva first shift back, huh?" Eve said, patting him on the back.

"A bit more exciting than I'd bargained for. Melissa's going to be fine, though."

His friends expressed how happy they were about that as they left the building. But Clay couldn't stop worrying about what had nearly happened. What could *still* happen.

They didn't know for sure who was after her, and why, despite their suspicions. Yes, she was fine for now.

But the next time, the bastard could very well succeed.

Charlene was, quite simply, an amazing woman.

Clay's mother was everything a mother should be, and everything Melissa missed about her aunt on a daily basis. She was immediately drawn to the woman's strength, tempered by a soft, disarming side that made her want to curl into her like a child and never let go.

She let Charlene take her to the older woman's house and steer her inside. There, the woman settled her on the sofa in the den and fetched her a cup of hot tea with honey. She wasn't normally a fan of hot tea, but just then it tasted like the best drink in the world. It soothed her, and she relaxed, trying not to mull over the horror of the truck taking a nosedive.

Of Shane, silent and still—

"Oh, honey." The sofa cushion dipped beside her, and the teacup was taken from her hand.

She hadn't even known she was crying until Charlene gathered her close, bringing her head to rest over her heart.

"Let it out, sweetie. I know how scared you were, believe me."

So she did. She let go of all the fear and pain, and gave it to this strong, sure woman who knew exactly what to do with it. She cried until she was sagging like a limp noodle, and Charlene continued to hold her, stroking her hair.

"Why is he doing this to me?" she whispered brokenly. But honestly, she knew the answer to that.

"Who, babydoll?"

"My Uncle James. He hates me. Always has."

"James Ryan is a piece of horse shit," the other woman said softly, surprising her.

Melissa pulled back and peered at Charlene's tight expression. "You know him?"

"I've lived in these parts all my life. Many of my childhood years were spent on a farm outside of town, and everyone knew about the Ryans. Not your parents, but James and his father, your great-uncle. The government's been trying to nail them for making illegal moonshine and God knows what else just about as long as it's been trying to balance the national budget—and they haven't been successful at either one yet."

Melissa had to snicker some at that. "True. So, James didn't start the business?"

"No, his father did, way back in the fifties. He'd built a nice little empire by the time he passed and left it to James. Your uncle saw it flourish from there, sort of like an out-of-control fungus."

This time, Melissa laughed outright. "Anything my uncle touches is rotten, for sure."

Charlene hummed in agreement.

"So, did you know my parents?" she ventured.

"No," the older woman answered, her gaze filled with warmth. "My family knew *of* them, and talk was they were nothing like their felonious family up in the hills. That's all I really knew of them."

She'd get nothing more there, and couldn't help but be disappointed. Part of her constantly sought some connection with her folks, but there just wasn't much left except faded memories.

"Rest awhile, and I'll make dinner in a bit." Charlene rose. "Come and I'll show you the guest room."

Melissa followed dutifully, then took off her shoes and sank into the soft, comfy bed with a sigh. Clay's mother smoothed her hair, then bent and kissed her cheek before straightening.

"Sleep, honey."

She couldn't help but obey, and knew nothing more for a very long while.

Clay hurried from the station the next morning as if the hounds of hell were after him.

As excited as he'd been to work his first shift, he

was ecstatic to see it end. All he cared about was getting to Melissa. He was sure his mother was sick of his constant texting to check on her, though she'd never say so. Every time, she'd replied that his lady love was still sleeping peacefully, having been quite drained from her ordeal.

He arrived at his mother's house right at seven thirty, parked, and rushed to the front door. His mom opened up before he could even knock, and he hugged her fiercely.

"How's she doing?"

"For the hundredth time, she's fine," his mother said in exasperation. But her eyes were sparkling, filled with love.

"Sorry. I've just been so worried."

"I know, honey. But she's up now, and a bit perkier than when you saw her last. Come on in, I've got breakfast ready."

His stomach rumbled, and he followed his mom inside. In the kitchen, Melissa was seated at the small breakfast nook table, sipping a mug of coffee. When she saw him, she got to her feet and walked right into his open arms.

"How are you, baby?" he asked, kissing her temple.

"I'm good, honestly. Hungry as hell, too, because I slept right through dinner last night."

"I'm sure you needed it. But now let's get you fed."

She sat and he helped his mom set the dishes on

the table. There was a bowl of scrambled eggs, bacon, gravy, and homemade biscuits. His belly growled again, and Melissa smiled.

"I'm not the only one who's starving."

"I could eat my weight in Mom's breakfast," he said, taking a seat. "Thanks for making all of this."

His mom grinned. "You know I love having someone to cook for, and now I have two people. Just promise you'll come over often."

"We will," he said.

Melissa spoke up. "But you have to let us bring something next time."

"I can probably do that." The other woman winked.

"Oh, Mom, the guys at the station are having a cookout at Howard and Kat's house this Saturday. You're invited, so Melissa and I can pick you up if you want to come."

"Oh, I don't know about that," she demurred. "I may leave the partying to you young people."

"We want you there. It's a welcome back party for me, and a bunch of hot firefighters want to spoil you," he teased. "How can you say no?"

"Well, when you put it that way!" She laughed. "I may come, then, but I'll drive myself and meet you there. That way I can leave when I want."

He figured she really just didn't want to be a third wheel with him and his girlfriend. Of course, she probably *didn't* want to stay up as late as his friends were known to party, he so it let it slide. "Sounds good."

They finished their breakfast, chatting companionably. He was happy to see that his mother had taken Melissa under her wing and that the two were getting along so well. Both women had been through so much turmoil in their lives, and had come out the other side, that they had plenty of common ground. They deserved to have each other.

After breakfast, he made Melissa sit while he helped his mom clean up and scrub the pans. When they were done, he was flagging some. He needed rest in his own bed, and it showed.

"Take your girl home, son. You need sleep."

"I will. We didn't get any calls last night, but you know it's never a deep sleep when we're always waiting for the alarm to sound."

"I know, baby."

"Thanks for everything, Mom. I love you." He wrapped her in his arms and gave her a noisy, sloppy kiss.

"Love you, too. Go on now, get!" she said, smiling.

The women hugged, then he ushered his lover out and settled her in his car. She fell silent on the drive to her place, and he kept an eye on her. Even though she'd slept well last night, now that she'd eaten her fill, she was sleepy again. Her eyes were drooping as she rested her head against the seat.

"I need a shower so bad," she said.

"Go, jump in and I'll take care of feeding the horses. I know how since you showed me."

"My poor babies! They're probably starving since nobody was home to feed them last night."

"I'm sure they're fine. You've got them fat as butterballs, and they've had grass and hay to munch on."

This seemed to placate her, and as soon as she went in to shower, he headed outside to take care of her "babies." All three were waiting in their usual spot, and if their greetings were any indication, they were mighty unhappy to have been left standing at their stalls with no grain.

"Sorry, guys," he said, crooning to them. "Who's hungry? Yeah, I'll get you fixed up in no time, don't worry."

He chuckled some at himself for talking to creatures that couldn't understand a word he was saying. Opening the side door to the feed room, he stepped inside and made his way over to the bins. There, he lifted the lid to the oats, and heard an ominous rattle. His hand froze in the act of reaching for the scoop.

There, coiled on top of the grain, was a large rattlesnake.

Fucking shit!

The serpent's head was bobbing in a raised position, ready to strike. Its tongue flicked, and it rattled again in warning.

Clay didn't move at first. Could barely breathe. His heart galloped a hard tempo in his chest, and sweat trickled down the side of his face. His eyes were locked with the snake's, and he knew the only two ways out of this were if the snake decided to leave, or he did.

So slowly he was barely moving, he began the tedious process of backing away. Centimeter by centimeter, until minutes later, he was able to finally move out of reach and look around for a weapon. His gaze found a hoe hanging on the wall, and he grabbed it.

He held the hoe out as far as possible, using it to fish the snake out of the grain bin. It was a huge fucker, probably six feet long. The thing dangled on the end of the hoe as he rushed outside and flung it into the grass. He wasted no time chopping its head off, and then sucked in several lungfuls of air, nearly hyperventilating at the thought of what had nearly happened.

"Jesus Christ," he said hoarsely, sagging against the side of the barn. His hand went over his heart as though to keep it inside his chest.

That damned thing could have bitten me. I could have died.

Oh, God. Someone put it there, thinking Melissa would be the one to feed the horses.

The truth hit him hard, and he cursed. The snake had definitely been placed there. The bin had been tightly closed, and no pests could have gotten in by themselves.

His hand shook as he hung the hoe back on the wall. Then he quickly fed the horses, gave them hay, and hurried back inside. He'd left the back door unlocked, and how he cursed himself for an idiot. The first thing he did was to check every nook and cranny of the house to make sure there were no other unwelcome visitors—scaled or human.

Satisfied the house was all clear, he walked back to her bedroom. She'd showered and was just finishing up with blow-drying her hair. The dryer went off and she placed it back under the sink, then turned to him as he parked his butt on her bed.

"There you are. What took you so long?" Her look of curiosity was replaced by concern. The ordeal must've shown on his face. "What's wrong?"

He blew out a breath. "There was a big fucking rattlesnake in the bin of oats."

Her eyes rounded. "What? How the hell did it get in there? Was the lid open?"

"No, it wasn't."

He recounted the story to her, and when he finished, she sat next to him and took his hand. He clasped it tightly and kissed her knuckles.

"I'm so glad it didn't get you," she said shakily.

"Me, too."

"My gut tells me that James is behind all of this. I'm going to get him somehow," she vowed, jaw clenching.

"I'd rather you just stay away from him and let the authorities deal with him. I don't want you anywhere near that asshole."

"I'd rather that too, but they haven't done a stellar job of collaring him so far."

Pulling her into his side, he tilted her head up and gave her a slow kiss. One that conveyed his emotions without saying a word. "Let's rest awhile, okay? Maybe things will be clearer when we wake up."

He wasn't sure about that, but it sounded good.

She let her towel drop to the floor and crawled into the bed. His cock stirred, but he doubted she wanted to be ravished right this second, after everything. He stripped and joined her, then situated her with her head resting on his chest. This was fast becoming his favorite position.

Sleep took him fast, and he sank with gratitude.

Sometime later, there was an insistent knock coming from the front of the house. The front door, he thought groggily. Glancing at Melissa, he saw that she was still sleeping and he didn't want to awaken her. So he extracted himself from her arms as carefully as possible and slipped from the bed. Once he'd pulled on his pants, he headed for the door.

He opened it to find an older man, possibly in his fifties, standing on the other side. The stranger was about six feet tall, graying brown hair. He stood straight, with an arrogant and intimidating air about him—and Clay immediately suspected his identity.

"Can I help you?" Clay asked in a barely civil tone. He eyed the batch of flowers clutched in the man's hands.

"I'm here to see my niece," the man said coolly. "And you are?"

"You first, since I'm the one who's actually welcome here."

The man's eyes narrowed. "I'm James Ryan, Melissa's uncle. Now that you have your answer, kindly fetch her for me. I haven't welcomed her to town, and we're long overdue for a visit."

His dismissive tone rankled. There was also something very dangerous lurking in that flat gaze. This wasn't a stupid man, or one to be underestimated.

"I don't think so," Clay replied in a cold voice. "Leave your number, and if she wants to talk with you, she'll call."

Anger tightened James's features. "And you are?" he repeated.

"I'm Clay Montana, the man who's standing between you and Melissa. And that's where I'm going to stay until she tells me different. So, get the fuck off her porch before I bodily remove you."

Clay thought the asshole would take a swing at him, so palpable was the rage on his face.

"Clay?" a soft voice said from behind him. "It's okay, I have something to say to my uncle."

The man's smirk didn't last long. Melissa came into the doorway, snuggling into Clay's side. It was a show of solidarity, that they were a couple. He draped his arm protectively around her shoulders as she had her say.

"Melissa, it's good to see—"

"Don't even bother to spout that lie, James," she hissed. "I know you're the one behind the attempts on me, so there's no reason for pretense between us."

"I only just heard on the news about you and your detective friend being run off the road by that van," he claimed, shaking his head. "I just came to make sure you're all right, and to give you these."

He held out the flowers and Melissa took them before Clay could voice a protest. Her expression never softened toward her uncle, however, and she continued to glare at him.

"That bullshit could fertilize a garden. You've never held any love for me, and you killed any I might've had for you long ago. You hate me because I'm a cop, and because I know your dirty secrets and I want proof of them to give to the Feds. That makes me a traitor in your eyes. Know this." Stepping from Clay's arms, she walked right up to the man and stuck her face into his.

"I know what you're up to, and I'm going to bring you down. I'm going to find enough on you to bury you so deep, parole will be a distant dream. Do you get that?"

James laughed, but the sound was devoid of real

mirth. "I get it, sweet niece. But you're wrong about me. I only want the best for you."

"Get your sorry, lying self off my porch, James Ryan," she spat. "And don't come back if you know what's good for you."

The gauntlet had been thrown down, and Clay had no doubt the man would pick it up. The evil was there, written on his face. James had no intention of backing down. He'd kill Melissa, first chance he got. Clay suppressed a shudder.

James spun and left, jogging to a Range Rover in the driveway. Melissa peered at it intently. As soon as the man had backed out and driven away, she marched inside. Clay followed, watching as she went into the kitchen and dumped the flowers in the garbage. Then she took a notepad and wrote something down on it.

"The make, model, and license plate number of his Range Rover," she said.

"Smart." He walked over to her, gathering her in his arms. "Are you okay, baby?"

"Yeah. I'm angry, but I'm all right. He infuriates me!"

"I know. He does the same to me. I can't imagine what living with him was like."

"He's so full of shit, and he *knows* I know it! That's what this little visit was about—he was trying to toy with me, let me know he's coming and there's nothing I can do to stop him."

"Except there is."

"Yes. I'm going to hang that bastard, and he's going to provide the rope."

Saturday, the day of Howard's cookout, dawned beautiful and clear. It was the perfect day for celebrating Clay's return to his team. For relaxing and getting to know his friends and their wives better.

Melissa wished they didn't have the specter of her uncle looming in the shadows, but for the moment it couldn't be helped. She pushed aside the thing that kept niggling in her brain about his visit, the wisp that she couldn't seem to grasp, and focused instead on having a good time.

Clay had been staying with her since she and Shane were run off the road, would barely let her out of his sight. She loved him for it, but they both needed this break.

She reveled in his playfulness as they got ready. They hadn't made love since the road incident, but she hoped tonight would be different. He was treating her as if she were made of glass, and that was going to stop. Sooner rather than later.

She could barely get dressed in her shorts and tank top with him squeezing her from behind and kissing on her neck. Giggling, she wriggled free and teased him back.

"You want some of this?" She jiggled her booty.

"Damn, woman! Let's just skip the party."

"Nuh-uh. There's this thing called anticipation. You're going to be so hot for it, you'll come in your pants at the party."

He arched a brow. "Think so? Hell, you're probably right. Though you'd better hope not because I don't rev back up as quick as I used to."

"Oh, baloney. I know that's not true." She leered at his crotch, making him laugh.

"Hey! I'm up here."

"Isn't that the woman's line?"

"I'm so abused."

"Sure, poor baby." Hugging him, she gave him a deep kiss, which he enjoyed with an appreciative growl before breaking their contact.

"Shit, if we don't leave now, I'm calling this whole thing off."

"Guess we'd better go, then."

Soon they were on their way. The drive didn't take long, and in less than fifteen minutes they were pulling up in front of a cute, modest house in an older neighborhood. The front sidewalk was lined with flowers, the yard neatly trimmed. Cars lined the street in each direction, a testament to the revelry going on in the back.

"Wow, they must have quite a get-together," she said.

"Nobody parties like a bunch of firefighters. You're about to experience either the most fun you've ever had, or the worst headache. There's not much in between with us."

"I'm sure I'll have fun. I've already met your team, and they're great."

"We'll see." He winked.

Taking her hand, he led her straight around to the back and through the gate in the fence. There, she saw . . . complete, joyful chaos.

A few of Clay's team were playing football, and some were lounging with beers. There were a few guys she didn't recognize, and Clay told her they were on other shifts at the station. There were plenty of wives, she assumed, but she didn't know any of them.

Six-Pack, who was manning the grill, waved them over. "Hey, come on over! Grab a beer!"

Clay had told her that the captain didn't drink, but it didn't bother him that all his buddies did. The others were doing their part to make up for the alcohol the big captain wasn't consuming, and much merrymaking was going on.

As they joined Six-Pack and retrieved beers from the cooler near him, Melissa saw the sign on the back fence that declared, *Welcome Home, Clay!* The warmth of his friends, their genuine happiness at having him returned to them, made her choke up a little.

She was instantly drawn into his world, fully and completely. The guys were fun and the women she met, Kat, Grace, Cori, Eve, and Shea Skyler, who she remembered was Shane's twin sister, were fantastic. Melissa had known about Shane's twin, but hadn't met the nurse before now, even though the woman worked in the ER at Sterling. Shea's husband, Tommy, she learned, used to be a firefighter at Station Five before he was injured and went to the fire marshal's office. Now he taught classes for the department, and seemed happy.

Tommy hugged Clay enthusiastically, and there were certainly no hard feelings that Clay had been moved to A-shift to fill Tommy's spot.

These people were incredible. Sure, from Clay she knew they all had flaws and each had been through their own brand of hell before they found happiness. But that made them even more real, and human, to her.

She made new friends, and laughed at their antics so often and hard her sides hurt. In all, it was the most perfect day ever . . . Because she suspected she'd found a large, exuberant extended family.

And she planned to hold on to them, and her man, with everything she had.

9

The party had been a roaring success, but Melissa was glad to be home.

Finally, she had her man to herself. They'd come back to her place and hopped in the shower right away, where he'd proceeded to stroke her until her body was a raging inferno.

"You're a beast," she told him.

"Is that good?"

"You're a *sexy* beast," she said, admiring his tight, fine ass as he bent over to dry himself. His skin gleamed with droplets, clinging to every lean muscle.

"I'll take that as a compliment, then." After he was dry, he tossed the towel aside, climbed into bed, and held out a hand. "Come here, baby."

Slipping her palm into his, she lowered herself to the bed and sat facing him. "I had a great time at the party today."

"I'm glad. I want you to like my friends."

"I love them," she assured him.

"Now, let's talk about something fun." His grin would've melted her panties—if she was wearing any. "Lie on your back and close your eyes."

Curious and excited, she did as he asked.

"No peeking."

"Okay."

She heard the nightstand drawer slide open and a rustling around. Next, his palm smoothed over her tummy, and down one thigh.

"Put your arms over your head and cross your wrists." She did. "Good. Now spread your legs wider, let me see all of you."

His sensual command plucked at her nipples like a physical touch and they hardened, as much from this game as from the night air on her damp body.

His palm traveled upward to her breasts, grazed the sensitized points as he spoke, low and mesmerizing. "Sweetheart, look at you, all spread and ready for me. I can do anything I want and you'll love it, isn't that so?"

"Y-yes." She wiggled a little, getting hot.

"You need it so bad, need me to do naughty things

to you. Whatever I want." His fingers found her sex, rubbing with just the lightest of touches, driving her crazy.

"Clay," she whimpered.

"Yes, baby? Need me to do something about that ache? God, you're wet."

His fingers disappeared and she heard a squirt. Then they returned, rubbing something slippery along her sex, all over her clit. As he rubbed, it warmed under his ministrations, transforming every spot on her body into a massive erogenous zone. She was lost to what he was doing to her, his control.

"Ooh." She moaned as a finger slipped inside, spreading the moisture.

She loved being bared to him, and this naughty play fired her blood. Seemed she wasn't alone.

Her nipples were pinched, oiled, and she arched her back with a gasp. He played with them for a few moments, and then moved between her spread thighs.

"Lift your legs and bend your knees, but keep your legs spread, out to the sides," he said, voice husky.

She complied, holding her knees, imagining what she must look like, offered to him this way. "I want to open my eyes so I can watch you."

"No. Keep them closed, just feel."

More oil dribbled on the exposed lips of her sex and he worked it over every crease, teased her throbbing clit. Some of the oil streaked downward, between her cheeks. His hand followed, smoothing the liquid all the way to her sex.

"Open to me," he murmured. "Trust me, give yourself to me."

His seduction was too much to resist. So wicked.

One well-oiled finger dipped inside her channel. Twisting slowly, stretching. She felt him move without removing his hand and suddenly his breath puffed against her slit.

"There you go, baby. You're all mine. So pretty, writhing on my hand, begging for more. And you do want more, don't you, my love?"

"Please, more!"

"More what?"

"Your fingers and your m-mouth. Clay . . ."

The feeling of fullness increased, burning a little, as he added a finger or two. It felt so good. Made her feel connected in more than a physical way.

Belonging to this man made her complete.

His hot tongue licked her slit. Just the tip and nothing more. Teasing, like a feather. Light enough to drive her insane as he worked her, turning her into a ball of mindless sensation.

"You want my mouth, honey?"

"Yes, dammit!"

His chuckle floated in the darkness. "Anything for my baby. You'll have my mouth, and I'm going to eat you until you come so hard you pass out. But I won't be finished with you just yet."

"Clay!"

"Know what I'll do to you next? I'm going to fuck you, honey. Right here," he said, twisting his fingers. "I'm going to fuck you until you scream, and you're going to come for me again."

With that, he lapped at her sex, tasting. True to his word, he ate her like a starving man, leaving no spot unattended. The storm built fast and she tried to hold back for a bit, but when he latched on to her clit and began to suck it like a piece of delicious candy, she came undone.

Forgetting about his order to keep her hands over her head, or not really caring, she reached down and buried her fingers in his hair. Her orgasm splashed over her in luxurious waves and she cried out, riding the pleasure.

When the last tremor subsided, she felt him withdraw, and reached for him automatically.

"I'm just getting myself ready. Not going anywhere. You can watch now if you want."

Melissa opened her eyes to see a pagan god kneeling near her feet. Keeping his gaze locked on hers, he fisted himself, making the shaft nice and slick.

He scooted forward and scooped his hands under her bottom. With little effort, he lifted her up. "Put your legs over my shoulders."

In this position, she was more exposed than ever, if possible. She loved being bared to him, for his pleasure. The languid haze spread to every limb once more, as if he had her enchanted.

Spreading her cheeks, he brought the head of his cock to her opening. Began to push, his face suffused with hunger.

"Oh!"

"Doing good, baby." More, inches at a time. "How do you feel?"

"Full," she moaned. "So full."

"Almost there. I wish you could see my cock splitting your pussy, claiming you." And then he was balls deep. "Ah, yes."

"Move, do something," she begged, clutching the sheets on either side of her body. "I need you."

He began to pump, slowly at first, letting her adjust. This was a fire that had never consumed her before and she was helpless as it built. Burned higher.

"Fuck, yeah. Sweetheart."

She thrashed, lost in how wonderful it was to be impaled on him. Owned by him. "Harder!"

Her demand flipped the switch and he gave her what she wanted. Fucked her with abandon, hips driving like a piston. Keeping her steady with one hand, he reached to her sex and massaged the tiny nub, relentless.

To her amazement, a second orgasm unfurled, shaking her apart. "Oh, fuck! Yes!"

Clay thrust deep and held there, throwing back his head with a hoarse cry. Heat warmed her inside, completing the circle. She'd never seen a man more beautiful in the throes of orgasm.

His cock twitched a few more times, and he gradually relaxed. Came down off the euphoric high and opened his eyes, smiling. "You were wonderful."

"Me? You're the gorgeous man who seduced me."

"Your man." He slipped out gently and stretched out beside her.

She rolled to face him. "You *are* my man." Reaching out, she touched his face. "And I love you."

His eyes widened and he snatched her into his arms, pulling her on top of him. "Say it again."

"I love you."

He laughed, the sound of sheer joy, and pulled her down for a lengthy kiss. When they broke away, he said, "I love you, too."

Yes, life was almost perfect.

The shadows could wait until tomorrow.

Monday pretty much sucked, as they tended to do.

The idyll of her long weekend with Clay had passed, and it was back to the grind. The day dragged on, and so did her cases. For hours, her thoughts strayed to her uncle and his visit. Something was still bugging her, something she couldn't put her finger on.

But she'd figure it out. She always did.

By the time she left, she was grouchy and tired. Clay was on shift, so he wouldn't return until seven the next morning, right before she had to leave for work again. Such was the life of being a firefighter's girlfriend, and the reality hit her more at that moment than ever before. Probably because things between them were serious. This was the real deal.

But she wouldn't trade Clay for anything. She loved him, and schedules sometimes clashed. They'd make it work.

At home that evening, she'd just popped a frozen dinner in the microwave when her cell phone rang. Picking it up from the counter, she saw that it was her nearest neighbor behind the far acreage of her property. She frowned. What was that about?

"Hello?" she said in greeting.

"Melissa, honey, this is Jane Fowler," the woman said.

"Yes, Jane, what can I do for you?"

"Well, it's what I can do for you," the woman replied wryly. "There's been some goings-on at the back of your property for a couple of nights now, and I thought I'd better let you know."

A chill gripped her heart, but she managed to keep her voice even. "What kind of activity are we talking about?"

"Lights. Vehicles. I've spotted at least two different ones. Not at the same time, though. Both were trucks, and they entered through a break in your fence at the back of your place where there shouldn't *be* a break. I don't know what these men are up to, but I didn't want your horses to find the spot and get loose."

"Thank you, Jane. I appreciate you letting me know."

"No problem. And Melissa, honey, don't go crawling around out there by yourself," the woman said with worry. "Call one of your detective friends to come over."

"Good advice. I'll do that. Have you noticed anything tonight?"

"Not yet, but it's a bit early. They've been showing up later."

"Okay. Thanks again."

"No problem. Us neighbors have to look out for each other."

Melissa ended the call and chewed her lip. Calling for backup was the best plan. But what if the trucks were nothing more than teenagers using her place to have a beer bash? Wouldn't be the first time.

Something told her the reason was more sinister. And that James Ryan was behind it.

She tried phoning for backup, but couldn't reach a single one of the guys. Shane was still healing and she didn't want to bother him. The others were either out or not answering.

"Fuck it, I'm a cop. I can find out what's going on by myself."

Outside, she saddled Biscuit, one of her brown mares. She wasn't as fast as the gray gelding, Boss, but his coat would shine at night like a beacon.

Before she mounted, she took stock. She had her cell phone, flashlight, and her sidearm in the holster at her belt. *I'm ready.*

Once she reached the back of the property, it didn't take long to find the cut in the fence. The bastards had left a hole large enough for a truck, or two, to pass through. She followed the tire tracks, and they seemed to disappear as they reached a small clearing.

Making a decision, she dismounted and moved Biscuit closer to her house, out of earshot but near enough to run to and ride home should she need the mare. Then she returned to the spot and waited.

She crouched low in the darkness, secure in her hiding place at the edge of the tree line where the rolling fields of her property met the thick woods. Kneeling in the newly green vegetation, she thanked God it was cool enough at night to keep the mosquitoes from launching a full-scale attack. She could only pray she wasn't sitting in something that would have her scratching miserable, hard-to-reach places for days.

She watched and waited. Yawned. Damn, this was boring, sitting out here playing detective on her own place. Probably for nothing, too. Since she'd committed herself to taking up the vigil tonight, the assholes probably wouldn't show.

Then, a low noise. The whine of a faraway engine, coming closer. She sat up straighter and leaned forward, peering into the night.

A pair of headlights topped the rise, cutting through the gloom. She could barely make out the shape as a pickup truck, which didn't help much. Three-fourths of the males in Cheatham County drove pickup trucks. Before she could move, another pair of headlights topped the hill following the first. *Two* trucks. Relief mixed with a healthy dose of anger spurred her into action. One truck? Maybe James's men. But two?

"Teenagers," she said, wishing she could be so sure.

Hopefully that's all there was to the suspicious activity Jane had seen. Kids coming out here to drink and raise hell where they wouldn't be discovered. They'd been a nuisance in the past, leaving beer cans and assorted litter in their wake. One of the drawbacks to inheriting her aunt's acreage well outside of town.

The taillights she'd been watching suddenly disappeared at the edge of the woods. Melissa suppressed a shiver. No lights meant they'd stopped and she couldn't see them anymore. She consoled herself with the knowledge that they couldn't see her, either. Not until she revealed her presence.

Creeping closer, she thanked God that the ground was soft and pliant under her boots. A few moments later she stopped even with the pickup trucks. No one seemed to be nearby, and a chill zinged down her spine. This wasn't right.

No blaring music, no teenage revelry.

Low, masculine voices snared her attention. A laugh in the darkness, harsh and crude. The glow of a cigarette and some other dim light deep in the woods ahead. The steady, muffled rhythm of something striking the earth, digging in.

A shovel.

Melissa knew the sound. Belatedly, she cursed herself for not holding out until one of the other detectives could accompany her. She was an idiot.

Keeping to the shadows, she moved ahead, skirting the area where the voices penetrated the air. At the center of the clearing, three men stood backlit by a heavy-duty halogen lamp. One man was bent over a shovel, a large black garbage bag on the ground at his feet, intent on his task while the other two watched.

Melissa squinted against the glare, but could only discern their forms. The men were of a strong, slim build, except for the one with the shovel. His shape was heavyset. One of the men watching wore a cowboy hat, but the other two were bareheaded.

"Did you two get the rest of the bags?" Cowboy asked the men beside him.

"We carried the last one, asshole."

Last one what? She was afraid to find out.

The heavyset man stopped digging. "Wait, he told us to—"

"Yeah, fuck *that*, and James. He ain't here stumbling through the woods at midnight with that fucking cop—"

"Shut up, moron," Cowboy snapped. Then to the heavyset man he said, "Let's just get it done. Who wants to run around all night hauling that and risk getting caught?" The heavyset man hesitated, then swore, pitching the shovel onto the ground. He pulled a flashlight from his back pocket and led the way, leaving the lamp on the ground. Melissa watched the trio move off into the darkness together, apparently to go fetch whatever they'd brought with them to dispose of.

Her attention went to the trash bag and she did a quick mental calculation of how long it might take them to make it to their vehicles and back. Five minutes, maybe less. Enough time to take a quick peek inside the bag to see what had them in such a hurry to complete the task for her uncle and get out of here.

She didn't like this. She should leave now and sneak back to the house. She should call Austin Rainey for help and he'd send someone. She could bring him back here when it was safe to see what the trespassers had left behind. Except . . .

They would be long gone by then and she would lose any chance of getting a better look at them and gather more evidence. Maybe she could circle around to the trucks and get the license plate numbers. She would investigate first, then ride for home and call Austin. Her mind made up, she stood on trembling legs and picked her way out of the brush.

In the small clearing, she knelt by the bag and glanced at the hole. What could the plastic contain that her uncle would want to bury it back here where the thing probably would never have been found? Drugs? Worse? Her mouth flattened into a grim line.

Fingers shaking, Melissa worked at the twisty tie, aware she'd wasted far too much time. She got the tie free, then slipped it into the front pocket of her shirt. The plan was to secure the bag afterward so they wouldn't be alerted that someone had been poking around. Opening the plastic, she shifted slightly to the side to allow the light from the lamp to illuminate the contents . . . and looked inside.

"Oh—*Oh my God.*"

There, in the bag, was the decomposing head of Officer Ron Nelson.

Just the head.

She shoved the bag away and shot to her feet, clamping a hand over her mouth to stifle the scream that wanted to escape. Bile rose in her throat, heart slamming so painfully in her chest she thought it might explode. She couldn't get sick. She had to get out of here. Now.

Never, until this moment, had she known how truly evil James Ryan was.

"Hey, bitch!"

"Who the fuck is that?"

Shouts and curses sounded behind her, bodies crashing through the woods. Survival mode kicked in, overriding the shock. She plunged headlong into the darkness and ran. Ran as never before.

A series of pops followed, pelting the trees and brush all around her. A stinging pain caught her near the left shoulder blade, but was lost in a burst of pure adrenaline.

Branches clawed at her face and arms, and she tripped over a rotting log. She went sprawling, the breath knocked out of her lungs, but sprung back to her feet and ran as though the very devil was in pursuit.

After a time she stopped and leaned against a tree, panting. Listened. She must've lost them, but wasn't taking any chances. Keeping to the cover of the woods, she made her way back to where Biscuit waited.

The shortest route home was over the fields, but she couldn't risk riding into the open. She'd have to go the long way, but at least they couldn't follow through the woods in their trucks. With any luck, they hadn't gotten a good look at her and didn't realize she was James's niece.

But that was a slim hope.

As she rode carefully through the trees, the burning agony in her shoulder penetrated her numb brain.

Switching the reins to her left hand, she reached up and felt her shirt. Sticky warmth soaked the front, and she felt the wet material clinging against her back as well.

Shot. The realization amazed her in a way that was strangely detached. Almost as if it had happened to someone else. A weird fog descended over her, and she recognized it as a serious warning signal. She needed help, fast.

Fighting to stay conscious became nearly impossible. Slumped in the saddle, Melissa let her mount guide them. When the horse stopped, it took her a full minute to realize she'd ridden into her backyard. The door leading into the mudroom was a mere ten feet away. It may as well have been a mile.

Melissa hoisted a leg over and slid out of the saddle, landing in a heap on the ground. Determined, she pulled herself upright by using the stirrup, then the edge of the leather seat. She couldn't pass out. If she did, she could very well die on her own lawn. Glancing around, she saw the three men hadn't intercepted her here. She was alone.

Aiming for the back door, she put one boot in front of the other. Her rubbery legs nearly gave out, but she kept walking until she reached her goal. Leaning against the wall for support, she dug the key out of her front jeans pocket, unlocked the door. She wobbled inside through the mudroom and into the kitchen, flipping on the light switch.

Phone? In her pocket.

She dug it out and made her way to the living room, collapsed on her sofa. Everything was distorted now. *Call Clay. Get help.*

Somehow she managed to punch his number. It rang three times. *Please, pick up.*

"Hey, baby! What's up? I miss you."

"Clay," she croaked. "Help me."

"What?" Fear colored his voice as he went on alert. "What is it? Has your uncle been back?"

"Shot," she whispered.

"Honey," he said, deadly calm. "It's going to be okay. Stay on the line, we're coming to you. Do you understand? Are you at home?"

"Yes."

A pause as he shouted to someone, maybe Six-Pack. More shouts, some at Melissa. She tried to answer, but her tongue was too big. Heavy.

Then she heard nothing at all.

Clay didn't recall much of the frantic race to Melissa's place.

He simply followed Howard's barked orders, knowing his captain had routed the call through dispatch, letting them know they'd received a plea from a gunshot victim. They were officially assigned to the call, and were making their way to her as fast as they were able.

His heart was a wild thing in his chest. Twice now

that murderous bastard had tried to take Melissa from him. But he wouldn't succeed. Clay wouldn't let him.

After what seemed like hours, they arrived in front of her house. Clay's throat ached to see one of the brown mares standing at the side of the house, saddled and riderless, reins dangling. They'd have to deal with her later.

Inside, his eyes searched frantically for her—and found her slumped on the sofa, eyes closed.

Blood. It was everywhere, coating her shirt and soaking the sofa underneath her. He cried out and rushed to her side, dropping to her knees.

"Baby?" he yelled, cupping her face. "Melissa! Answer me!"

A strong hand gripped his shoulder, pulling him back. Howard's voice rumbled, "You're not helping, so get out of the way. Right now!"

Resisting the urge to fight back was tough. But he knew his captain was right, and moved back to let them help her.

After an interminable wait while he paced, they had her on the gurney with an IV and heart monitor attached. "She's stable," Six-Pack said. "But she's lost a lot of blood, and we need to get her rolling."

Nobody said a word as Clay climbed in the back next to her, opposite his captain. Tears coursed down his face unchecked, but he didn't care. Nothing mattered except making sure she got help, and was okay.

"You're all right, baby," he said over and over, holding her hand. "You're fine. I'm here. I love you."

Howard said nothing, just did his job, taking good care of her until they arrived at Sterling.

There, she was whisked away and he wasn't allowed to follow. He was far too close to the situation and there was nothing to do but wait. He thought about calling his mother, but wanted to hear some news first. Charlene had been though so much and he didn't want her sitting here for hours and getting exhausted.

The station didn't get another call, so the guys waited patiently for news with him. He loved them for that, and no words needed to be spoken. They had his back, always.

A uniformed officer showed up to question them, and it didn't take long for the news to filter to Melissa's colleagues. Soon the waiting room was filled with detectives, and the big auburn-haired police captain from the other day.

"Family of Melissa Ryan?" a doctor called.

Austin stepped forward with the confidence he wore so well. "I'm Captain Austin Rainey, and Melissa Ryan is one of my detectives. She has no family, and as this pertains to an ongoing case, I'll need a full briefing of her condition."

All of that wasn't strictly true, but the doctor was swayed by the preponderance of evidence before him—the presence of half the police force.

"Very well, come this way." Apparently the doc's courtesy didn't extend to allowing everyone to eavesdrop.

A few minutes later, Austin returned and headed straight for Clay. The others kept a respectful distance, but their ears were open.

"She's going to be fine," was all Rainey had to say.

Clay's knees buckled, and someone pushed him into a chair. More hands pushed his head between his knees to keep him from passing out. A few moments later, he was able to sit up without spots dancing in front of his vision. Austin sat beside him, Howard on the other side.

"The wound was clean, in the fleshy part of her upper shoulder," Austin continued. "In and out. Looked much, much worse than it was in reality."

"Thank God. When can I see her?"

"The doc said to give her an hour or so in recovery, then they'll get her settled into a room. He said she probably wouldn't have to stay more than a day or two, which is good. Admitting her is just a precaution, really."

Clay nodded, grateful beyond words. But he had to say something to Rainey and his friends. "Thank you for finding out."

"Hey, it was selfish on my part. I think Melissa's very special and I wanted to be sure she was all right."

Clay nodded and turned to Six-Pack and his team.

"Thanks, guys. I lost my cool, and I wasn't going to be any help. I don't know what I'd do without you."

"You're stuck with us," Jamie piped up. "So you don't get to find out."

The others chuckled and Clay allowed himself a small smile. She was going to be fine. That was all that mattered.

"Hey, sleepyhead."

Clay watched as Melissa's eyes blinked open and regarded him in confusion. "What?"

The question came out sort of garbled and he smiled, kissing her on the forehead. "Seems you had a run-in with some nasty characters. When you're more awake, Austin and your team are here to find out what happened, okay?"

She nodded, trying to sit up, and then grimaced. "Ow! Shit."

"Easy there. You took a bullet through the fleshy part of your shoulder. In and out, I was told. No permanent damage."

"That's good." She frowned, her senses slowly returning. "I remember what happened."

A rock formed in his gut. "Want me to get Austin?"

"Not yet. Want to sit here and wake up for a few."

"Anything you want, baby. I'm not going anywhere."

She clutched his hand, and after a couple of minutes, tears started running down her cheeks.

"Hey, you're okay. Why the tears?" He brushed them away but they kept falling.

"They killed him. Or at least they were getting rid of him for whoever did. Probably my uncle."

His blood ran cold. "Who?"

"Get Austin in here for me now, would you? And my guys, too."

"Sure. Be right back." After kissing her, he left the room and rounded up her team. They followed, eager to hear what she had to say, yet dreading it at the same time.

He knew, because he felt the same.

"Melissa, how are you feeling?" Austin said, moving close to take her hand.

"Well, I'm alive. That's something, considering."

"We're so glad you're awake," Shane said, smiling. He was still recovering from his concussion, but nothing would have kept him away. Taylor, Chris, and Tonio echoed his words as they crowded in.

"I'm glad you guys are here," she said, appearing touched by their concern. "I need to tell you what went down. The quicker we catch my uncle, the better."

"Take your time," Taylor told her.

She took a deep breath. "My neighbor, Jane Fowler, called earlier to tell me there had been prowlers at the back of my property the past couple of nights and I needed to check it out."

"And you went to investigate on your own," Tonio growled. "Why didn't you call somebody?"

"I tried, but no one answered! Anyway, I went and I can't change it." She shuddered. "I found more than I bargained for."

"What, or who, was that?" Austin asked. "Your shooters?"

She nodded. "Yeah. They were there to bury something at the back of my property, and they were doing it for my uncle. They said his name."

They waited, and Clay felt sick. "What was it, baby?"

"The head of Officer Ron Nelson."

10

Melissa watched Clay's face turn gray, and her team looked just as sick as she felt.

"Just his head?" Taylor muttered. "Fucking hell. The poor bastard."

"I couldn't believe it, even though I was afraid they were there for no good reason. I didn't expect it to be Ron, exactly, but I knew it wouldn't be good. There were three men, and they were talking about burying something for James."

"Did they mention his last name?" Shane asked.

"No," she said with regret. "I wish they had. James is a common name, and even though we know it's my uncle, that's not proof."

"Can you describe them?" This from Tonio.

She did, plus what she'd seen of the trucks, which wasn't much help. It was dark, and she hadn't seen much very clearly. "But Ron's face? I saw that clear as day." Sudden urgency shot through her. "You've got to get some guys out to my place! They could go back anytime and remove the evidence!"

"I'm on it," Austin said, standing. Palming his cell, he left the room.

"What purpose would your uncle have for targeting your property, specifically?" Shane asked thoughtfully. "You said the neighbor had noticed activity for two nights previous."

"Yes. I think they did that to draw my attention to the crime, and they wanted me to find Ron's body."

"How do you figure?"

"This is James Ryan we're talking about. If he wanted the body to remain hidden, he's got the entire countryside around us where he could've ditched Ron and his body never would've been found. But he gets my attention, and dumps it on my place."

"To prove he can get to you," Taylor said in disgust.

"Exactly." She sighed. "He couldn't have planned that I'd actually catch them in the act, or that his men would shoot me. By now he's wishing they'd aimed better."

"That's not funny," Clay said, looking upset.

"Wasn't meant to be."

Clay took her hand, kissing it. He seemed to need

constant contact, and that was fine by her. She needed him, too.

Austin came back a short time later and said, "I have two officers on the scene right now. They just arrived at the area and confirmed that the bag with Officer Nelson's head is still there." He looked as though he wanted to vomit as he went on.

"There were a few other bags scattered around, and they believe those contain the rest of Nelson's body parts. The men were probably supposed to bury them all over your place and keep us busy for days. As it is, I'm hopeful they didn't manage to do their job, and we can give his widow closure."

Melissa felt horrible for the man's wife. And equally horrified that Ron had suffered such a terrible death just because her uncle was evil and out to get his niece.

"You're not to blame for this," Clay said quietly, as though he'd read her mind. "None of it."

"That's true," Austin put in. "Wipe that thought out of your mind."

She swallowed hard. "It's tough to remember that. Especially now."

There wasn't much more to say. The distress of the situation, and her injury, had worn her out. Her lids got heavy and she yawned.

"Sleep." Clay kissed her cheek. "I'll be here when you wake up."

She shut her eyes and let the terror drift away.

* * *

Three weeks. Three miserable weeks, two of them recovering from the wound that was stubbornly taking its time to heal and for the tenderness to fade.

Three weeks of wanting to slice and dice her uncle's balls and give him a taste of his own medicine.

The two weeks off weren't all bad, she had to concede. Clay and Charlene had taken turns babysitting her the first week after she'd been released. The second week Melissa had put her foot down and declared her independence once more. Clay was welcome to stay over at her place, but only as a lover—not a damned nursemaid.

Grinning, he'd agreed and backed off, for the most part. When he forgot and tried to intervene, babying her too much, all she had to do was give him a pointed glare. He'd walk away whistling, stating he was just happy she was feeling well enough to be *bitchy*—er, *assert herself*.

The lovable jerk.

Today, he was home and feeling rather horny if the rod in his shorts was any indication. She went to find him and located him in the kitchen, rummaging in the fridge for a snack. Grinning, she sneaked up behind him and reached between his legs, cupping his balls through his shorts.

He yelped and spun around, then laughed. "Oh, it's like that, is it?"

"It is," she declared, winding her arms around his neck. "Make love to me, fireman."

"That's a demand I can't refuse."

With a gleam in his eye, he pulled her into the living room.

"Oh, Clay. Make love to me," she whispered. "*Now.*"

They stripped quickly, clothing flying in all directions.

What he'd done to deserve such a priceless gift as Melissa, he didn't know. In wonder, he skimmed his palms down the graceful curve of her neck, to her slim shoulders, careful to avoid bumping her freshly healed wound. He brushed his fingers across the swell of her breasts, her puckered little nipples. His lady.

He rolled the taut peaks between his fingers, pinching them lightly. Bracing her weight with her hands flat on the floor, she leaned back into the front of the sofa, spreading those long legs. Offering herself to him.

He groaned, drinking in her natural beauty as his heart pounded in anticipation. Three weeks of abstinence was forever, and he was ready. She was all silvery skin, curves of breasts, and lean hips, the dark nest of curls at the vee of welcoming thighs.

His erection was curved toward his stomach, hot and hard. Throbbing to the point of real pain. Already, a drop of cum beaded at the head of his penis.

He was eager to be buried deep, to shoot inside her heat.

Smiling, she wrapped her fingers around his erection, stroked, swirled the pearly drop around the head of his penis. He gasped at the wonderful, wicked bolt of desire sweeping him.

"Melissa, I'm not going to last," he croaked. "I can't—"

"Shh, it's okay. Don't hold back."

Her tongue laved the tip, licking away the sticky wetness as she continued to pump his shaft. He shuddered, balls tightening, the heat rising in his loins, on the verge of losing control too soon. Her other hand found his sac, kneaded gently, and his breathing hitched.

Unable to help himself, he let his gaze drift down to watch. The sight nearly undid him. Beautiful Melissa, kneeling between his spread legs. Working his cock with her silky touch, her warm, wet little mouth. Taking obvious enjoyment in reducing him to a mindless puddle. Demanding all of him.

Oh, yeah. She can have me. Whenever, however she wants.

She took his length deep, sheathing his cock to the very base. He buried his hands in her wild hair, closing his eyes in ecstasy. *Hers now. All hers.*

"Melissa . . . oh, fuck!"

He pumped his hips slowly, in tandem to the pull

of her sweet mouth. She sucked eagerly, teeth scraping, tongue sweeping the ridge of his penis. So damned good. He wanted more. Harder, deeper. How could she take all of him? He never wanted to hurt her.

Then he wasn't capable of thinking anymore. She grabbed his hips, urging his thrusts. There was nothing but the rising throb of heat threatening to burst him into a million shards. Blow him apart.

He gave himself over to the woman he loved.

With a hoarse cry, he stiffened. Shot into her throat, pumping on and on. Riding the waves crashing through him until he stood trembling on legs that barely held him upright.

When the last of the aftershocks had faded, she released him and wiped her mouth with the edge of her discarded shirt. She looked at him with a saucy grin, and his heart turned over.

Love swelled in his chest, and fierce protectiveness. Given the chance, he'd send that son of a bitch uncle of hers straight to hell.

"Mmm," she purred, slanting him a sexy look. "I loved doing you. You've corrupted me."

"Then I'll consider my job well done."

She laughed. "I love you, Clay Montana."

Joy burst in his soul. "I love you more, baby."

She was a miracle.

Taking her chin, he kissed her. Reveled in the dark

flavor of himself on her lips. Him, and no one else. Ever again. The knowledge aroused him all over again, his softened cock waking anew.

He laid Melissa back gently on the floor, following her down. Cradling her, he pressed butterfly kisses to her lips, nose, chin, forehead. She rested a hand on top of his head, running his hair through her fingers, and he loved the sensation.

Dipping lower, he turned his attention to her breasts. Capturing one tight pebble in his teeth, he groaned, sucking it. Feasting like the starving man he was. She arched into him, gripping his head, gasping encouragement. He swirled one peak, then the other, as one hand skimmed down her flat belly.

His fingers found the springy nest of fiery curls, and lower still, to her wet sex. Her thighs parted for him, hips urging his touch. He stroked the hot, sensitive nub, the pouting lips, slick and ready for him. Suckled her breasts, teased her clit until she writhed, unable to take any more.

"Clay, please," she moaned, yanking his hair. "I need you inside me."

He needed no further encouragement. Positioning his body over hers, he guided the tip of his cock to her moist opening. Worked it in slow, making certain he wouldn't hurt her.

And in one long, delicious stroke, pushed deep. Her tight sheath gripped his cock with silken heat. She clutched his shoulders as he began to pump in as far as possible, his balls rubbing against her bottom. God, he always relished the feeling of being buried inside her. Then out, inch by wicked inch. Skin deep, inside her again. Wanting to crawl in and never come out. Fusing their souls.

Never, ever anything like this. The power of their connection shook him. Humbled him. She was a gift, a treasure. Mindful of her healing shoulder, he held her close, making sweet love to her. That's what she deserved, and he gave her all the love he had.

Her nails dug into his back. "Oh, yes, yes. Faster!"

He came undone, clutching her tight, thrusting hard, their bodies slapping together. Hot, blazing, burning him up. Higher and higher. Gonna explode . . .

"Come with me, baby," he demanded.

Hips bucking, she cried out. Her release shattered him. Seated deep, he let her carry him over the edge, into oblivion. Her orgasm milked his cock as he spurted into her, harder than before. More than he'd thought possible.

"You're perfect in every way," he said.

"No, we're perfect, together."

"You couldn't be more right about that."

He held her for a very long time, right there on the floor.

Melissa sat at her desk, back on duty. Full duty, for the first time in four weeks.

It was a mixed bag of good and bad. She was glad to get back to work, but more than a bit frustrated by the lack of anything solid on her uncle.

She stared at a series of reports on her desk. These were the vehicles that their surveillance had seen coming and going from her uncle's compound.

A few were trucks that the three henchmen with Ron's body could've been driving. One of them was a white utility van—and it was dented in the front, with black paint on the grill. Her uncle was arrogant not to get it fixed.

They'd gotten the plates of each vehicle. Now all they had to do was wait.

"You're going down, you fucker," she seethed. "I'm gonna put you away."

If it was the last thing she did.

11

A while later, Melissa rubbed her tired eyes, trying to concentrate on a different case file. An eighty-year-old had walked away from a nursing home, and no one could find him. The area outside the city was so fraught with hazards for a confused elderly person—the Cumberland River, the hills and forest—that she feared what had become of him.

"Melissa, something just came through," Shane said, hurrying into the office. He was carrying a piece of paper from the printer. "The plates on the van that we suspect ran us off the road came back registered to a man named Joe Henson. He's got an apartment here in town."

"Joe. Not my uncle," she said thoughtfully.

"No, though I know you were hoping it was your uncle's van."

Sitting back in her chair, she thought about that. "Big Joe. He's one of my uncle's henchmen, has been for a long time. I'm betting the apartment is just a cover. Unless he's moved, he lives on the compound, always has."

Shane's eyes gleamed with the anticipation of the hunt. "I'll get a warrant for his arrest, attempted murder of a police officer."

"He may not have been the one behind the wheel."

"If he wasn't, he'll know who was, and I'm betting it was your uncle. Either way, we'll be able to get warrants to search both his apartment *and* the compound."

Something niggled in her brain once again. That elusive detail about her uncle's visit . . .

She sat up straight. "He was talking about the van!"

"What?" Shane looked confused.

"My uncle! The day he came to see me, he mentioned the van that hit us," she said, holding Shane's gaze. "Said he saw the story on the news." She saw the instant he got it.

"We never released what *type* of vehicle hit us!" he crowed.

"That's it! This is what we needed," she exclaimed in excitement. "We needed a way onto that compound, and my uncle being stupid enough mention the van, plus to use it and Joe to do his dirty work, just gave it to us!"

"We need to be careful. The armed guards around that place may not let us close."

"Oh, they will. Because I'm going to let my uncle know I'm coming."

As she'd expected, James Ryan wasn't able to just ignore his niece throwing down the gauntlet. His pride and meanness wouldn't let him.

"I'll be waiting," he'd sneered, and cut off the call.

As she rode in the first of three cars full of detectives and officers, a shiver passed through her. Was she making a huge mistake? She hadn't even called Clay to let her know this was going down, and he'd be furious.

Please forgive me. I have to see this through.

Her uncle's attempts on her life wouldn't go unanswered. Even if they found not one shred of evidence, he would know that she refused to be cowed.

As they wound through the hills, sliding deeper into his territory, however, a chill of trepidation took root and grew. If she fucked this up, more lives than hers were at stake. Her entire team and several officers were putting themselves at risk to protect one of their own, to bring her would-be killer to justice.

She couldn't help but think she'd played right into her uncle's hands.

At last the road ended at a huge, imposing metal

gate. It had to be at least ten feet tall, and there were two men flanking either side of it. Both of them were armed with rifles. The weapons remained slung across their backs, but the threat was clear enough.

Fuck with us, and cops or not, nobody will find your bodies.

"Jesus," Shane said quietly.

Taylor snorted. "No shit. This is like something out of *Deliverance*."

"Worse," Melissa told them. "Keep your eyes open and your trigger finger ready."

After peering into each vehicle, one of the men got on his cell phone and walked a few paces away, talking into the device. When he was finished, he ended the call and the gate started opening slowly. He waved them through with a smirk.

"I feel like I've gone through a travel warp and landed in a South American country," Taylor said. "Complete with drug lords." He looked out the window, jaw ticking with nerves.

Nobody replied. The tension in the car could be cut with a knife. The feeling that she'd made a terrible mistake was growing worse, but it was far too late to turn back. What else was she supposed to do, though? Just let her uncle's attempts go unanswered until he finally succeeded?

Moments later, several large buildings came into view. The place hadn't changed much, except it had expanded. "That's the main residence, though it looks more like a warehouse," she said, pointing. "And there's the main distillery behind it, off to the left. The other buildings store their finished product, grain, weapons, food supplies, you name it."

Taylor was right—the compound *was* like a small country.

Shane parked their car in front of the residence, and they got out. Tonio and Chris were in the car behind them, and four officers in the one behind that. All to serve a couple of warrants. Christ Almighty.

She was glad Captain Rainey had taken the danger seriously.

The compound was eerily quiet as she, Shane, and Taylor approached the big front door. Their weapons were holstered, but unclipped, and they were wary. Melissa knocked, and waited. And they waited some more. It was nerve-racking because James had to know they were there. He was trying to make them nervous, and it was working.

At last the door opened, and her uncle was standing there wearing a smug smile. He was dressed in jeans and a white T-shirt with a plaid long-sleeved shirt over it. She'd lay money he was carrying a gun, probably underneath the plaid shirt.

He wasn't physically as imposing as she remembered from childhood. He was bulky but not fat, and not as tall as Clay. His salt-and-pepper brown hair was longish, and he sported a full beard now, unlike the day he'd come to see her. His dark eyes assessed them shrewdly, and his stance was relaxed. He wasn't the least bit intimidated—they were on his turf.

This wasn't some ignorant hillbilly, and they'd all do well to remember that.

"Well, look who it is," he drawled. "The prodigal daughter returned home. Should I have thrown a party? Don't know where I'd find balloons to match that particular color of blue you're wearing."

She wasn't in uniform, but his meaning was clear. As was the unspoken threat. Beside her, Taylor and Shane shifted.

"Hello, James," she said coolly. "It's been a long time since I've set foot here."

"Too long. I'm hurt that you didn't visit sooner." His tone said just the opposite.

"I'm touched. But I think we both know I'm not here to socialize. I have a warrant to search the property, and another one for the arrests of you and Joe Henson for attempted murder. If Joe is here, I suggest you urge him to give himself up peacefully and that you do the same."

His expression showed no surprise at the information. "He's not here. Don't know where he is, haven't seen him for a few days. He probably took off."

He was lying, she was sure of it. "Be that as it may, we still have a warrant for a search. James Ryan, you're under arrest for—"

Her uncle laughed out loud, as though she'd told

the funniest joke he'd ever heard. "Sure, sure. You and your friends can arrest me, and go right ahead and look. What's it matter to me? You'll find nothing."

She stared at him, uncertain. If he planned to let them search without a fight, he'd either swept the place clean, or he never planned to let them leave alive.

She figured it was the latter.

"Go ahead," James said, waving a hand. "Take a look. Not that it will matter."

"You're under arrest. Don't move." Handing her uncle the search warrant, she quickly cuffed his hands in front of him. Then she stepped off the porch and led the men far enough away so James wouldn't overhear.

"I'd leave one of the uniforms with him to keep an eye on him," she suggested. "Then I think we should search the small outer buildings first. That's where he keeps some of his treasures, like guns and drugs. I also know a place in the woods beyond those buildings were he hides things. Or used to anyway."

"Sounds good," Shane said. "Lead the way, and then we'll spread out."

She did, keeping a sharp eye on their surroundings. The silence was weird, especially in a place that was normally crawling with people. She and the others fanned out and started searching. Minutes later, just as she finished looking through one small empty outbuilding, she heard Shane call out.

Walking outside, she spotted him stamping through

the forest about forty yards away. He pointed to something farther in the trees.

"I think I found the van," he shouted.

That was all he had time to say before all hell broke loose. Gunfire erupted, followed by shouts and men emerging from nowhere. A bullet thudded into the wall too close to her head, and she ducked around the corner, drawing her weapon with a curse. She'd known her uncle wouldn't just let them nose around the property. He'd only been playing with them.

Peering around the corner, she saw a gunman take aim at Shane. Quickly, she fired off a couple of rounds, and the man fell to the ground, unmoving. Shane was darting from tree to tree, trying to remain out of the line of fire.

This was it. The war was on, and she was determined not to let James win. If he did, he'd be sure to hide their bodies where nobody would ever find them. The authorities would never pin a thing on him.

The battle was fierce. Melissa moved carefully around the perimeter of the compound, covering her friends and taking out as many of her uncle's men as she could. Unbearable minutes passed, listening to the gunshots, screams of pain, wondering if any of those voices belonged to her team.

Then, disaster.

Tonio was crossing from one building to another when a man stepped around a tree and opened fire.

Before Melissa could swing her weapon toward the enemy, Tonio's body jerked as he went down in a hail of bullets.

"No!" she screamed, firing several rounds at the bastard. He went down as well, and didn't move.

Tonio wasn't moving, either. Melissa made her way toward him as fast as she dared, watching the area for more shooters. Finally she reached the big man's side, and crouched, noting several bullet wounds in his torso and one in his right thigh. His eyes were closed, and she couldn't tell if he was breathing.

"Tonio? Oh, God."

Grabbing him under his arms, she began to drag him backward. Suddenly she had help as Chris skidded to a halt beside them.

"Here, give him to me!" Chris took over, slinging his partner over his shoulder in a fireman's carry and jogging for the relative safety of the trees. She followed, pulling out her cell phone to call dispatch.

When she connected, she wasted no time identifying herself. "Officer down! Detective Salvatore has been shot! We're at the Ryan compound, and we need an ambulance! We're under heavy fire!"

Dispatch promised backup and an ambulance as fast as they could get them there. After hanging up, she turned her attention back to Tonio. Chris was ripping open his shirt—and let out a cry of sheer relief.

"A vest! He's wearing a vest, thank God." He ran

a hand through his hair. "Most of the shots hit the vest, but he's got one wound high on his shoulder, and the one on his thigh as far as I can see."

"Doesn't look like they're bleeding too heavily," she said. "I'm glad as hell he was protected. I'm wearing mine, but I wasn't sure about him."

"Me, too."

Tonio sucked in a harsh breath and groaned, coming around. "What the fuck happened?"

"You nearly got turned into a spaghetti strainer, that's what," Chris told him. "Your vest saved your ass."

"Feels like I got hit by a truck."

"Just stay still, okay?" Melissa told him. "Help is on the way."

Tonio didn't have the breath to argue. Looking up, Melissa scanned the area and saw a lone figure slipping into a side door at the main distillery.

"Stay here with your partner," she told Chris. "I'm going after James."

"Be careful!"

"Will do."

If that evil son of a bitch thought he was going to get away from here, he'd better think again. *I'm coming for you, and you're going to pay.*

Finally.

The call came in at 7:08 p.m.

Officer down, and an ambulance needed ASAP. But

that wasn't all. There was a major shootout taking place at a compound outside of town, and the potential for casualties on both sides was high. Three companies were being dispatched, but they were to remain outside the perimeter until the danger was past.

His heart stuttered as fear washed over him. Was Melissa one of the wounded? Please, no. *I've waited all my life for her, and nothing can happen to her now. I won't survive it.*

Why hadn't she called, told him where she was going?

For this very reason. She knew she'd be in danger and didn't want me to worry.

"You drive," Six-Pack said to Clay, and tossed him the keys to the ambulance. "You're ready to get back on that horse. Let's go save some lives."

He swallowed hard, and nodded. "Let's go."

Clay drove through town, and couldn't help but shudder as he recalled the last time he'd been behind the wheel of the vehicle. Julian was in the passenger's seat, just like that day. But not quite.

This time was different. The call he was rushing toward involved someone he loved. Nothing compared to the urgency he felt to get to her.

Outside a huge gate, they were met with a sea of lights belonging to police cars. They were ordered to wait, which went against the fiber of his very being. People were injured, maybe Melissa, and standing around was hell.

He heard the gunshots. Each one was a strike against his nerves, ramping up his fear for his love. They seemed to be lessening in frequency, a pop here and there.

Clay walked up to an officer. "What's happening? Do we know who the injured officer is?"

"No, sir. I'm afraid not," he replied, his body tense. "We're still waiting on the go-ahead to let you in there."

On the heels of that statement, a huge explosion rocked the earth as a fireball shot into the sky.

"Holy fuck!" someone cursed.

Cold terror gripped his insides. The blaze shot into the sky, spewing fire and black smoke like a rampaging dragon intent on devouring everything it its path. *Please let her be safe. Please.*

"Okay, we've got the all-clear," Six-Pack shouted. "Let's move in!"

That meant the cops had James and his men subdued, right? He drove through the gates, keeping an eye out for any familiar cops. Especially one in particular.

The scene in the compound was total devastation. Bodies dotted the lawn, some men past any help. Some were writhing, moaning in pain. In the background, several buildings burned. He'd never seen anything quite like this.

His team and Station Two turned their hoses on the blaze while Clay helped others attend the wounded.

He heard a shout and looked up to see Shane and Chris carrying Tonio Salvatore between them. The man was conscious and grimacing in pain.

"Tonio!" Julian yelled, running to his brother. "Where are you hit?"

"Shoulder and leg," he rasped. "It's not that bad. My chest hurts worse because of the rounds stopped by my vest."

"*Madre de Dios!*" Julian appeared ready to pass out from the knowledge that he'd almost lost his brother.

The ambulance crew from Station Two intervened smoothly. "You can't treat your own brother," one of them said. "You're too shaken. We'll take over with the detective."

"Thank you," Julian managed, though he didn't appear happy about stepping aside. To Tonio, he said, "I'll see you later, at the hospital."

"Sure thing, bro. Remember, I'm fine. Okay?"

"Yeah." Julian sent the other man a half smile. But he was still rattled.

"Where's Melissa?" Clay asked Shane and Chris after they'd relinquished their fallen detective. Dread gripped him when they glanced at each other uneasily.

"I'm not sure," Shane said. "She went after her uncle. We were busy with Tonio and I haven't seen her since the fire started."

"We're going to look right now," Chris added.

The two men jogged off, starting their search.

Looking around, Clay saw things were under control for the moment. He couldn't wait another second to find Melissa. He had to know if she was alright.

Jogging for the main buildings, he chose the direction the other detectives hadn't gone. They'd find her faster if they spread out. Hopefully he could avoid getting in trouble by claiming he was looking for more victims—which was mostly the truth.

"Melissa!" he shouted. Again and again, he looked. Methodically, he searched each of the buildings, only to find dead men. There was one injured, and he had to carry that victim back to his crew before resuming his search.

Pausing outside a side door to a large building, one of the only ones not yet on fire, he heard loud voices coming from inside—and one of them belonged to a woman. Heart pounding, he quietly pushed his way inside and followed the sounds of the voices raised in anger. Keeping to the shadows, he crept forward and saw Melissa and her uncle in a standoff.

The man was holding a lighter; both of them were armed with their weapons pointed at each other. The sight froze his blood. There were large containers everywhere, and the unmistakable aroma of fermenting alcohol. The asshole was methodically setting his facilities on fire, probably to get rid of the evidence.

"How did you get the cuffs off?" Melissa asked him, her tone angry.

He held up the broken links. "One of my men obliged me by shooting them."

"What do you hope to accomplish? You'll still have to answer for attempting to murder a police officer."

"Not if I get rid of you along with the evidence," he sneered at her.

"We're at a stalemate, James. Drop the weapon." She adjusted her grip. "You can get out of this alive."

"Oh, I know I can. It's you who won't."

He took a shot, and Melissa dove to the floor, returning fire. As he ducked for cover behind a large tank, she scrambled to get around him for a better shot. Clay was trying to make his way toward her when James opened fire again, hitting a tank and puncturing the side. Liquid began to spill onto the floor and spread, a recipe for disaster.

As they traded shots, Clay noted that the liquid had spread to where her uncle was standing, and he didn't seem to notice. One spark, and this place was going up in flames.

He'd almost reached her when his fears came to fruition.

One of Melissa's shots hit a tank and ricocheted, creating a spark. The spark became a flame that grew and ignited with a whoosh—and shot toward the spot where her uncle stood.

Instantly the man was engulfed in flames, and his screams reverberated in Clay's brain. Burning alive was one of the most horrible deaths imaginable. He couldn't bring himself to feel too sorry for the ass-hole, but he wished Melissa didn't have to see it.

Just as James crumpled to the floor, Clay grabbed her hand and yanked her to his chest. "Thank God you're okay!"

"Where did you come from?" she gasped.

"We got called out. He's set fire to a lot of the build-ings, plus there's plenty of injured, including Tonio."

"How is he?"

"He'll be okay, but we have to get out of here," he urged, pulling her with him toward the door. "Those stills are going to go any second!"

Behind them, the fire became another living dragon as they raced toward the door. Clay pushed her outside ahead of him as a great whoosh sounded. The whole area seemed to hold its breath. He grabbed her from behind, was taking her to the ground, cov-ering her with his own body, and then—

BOOM.

The blast hit his back with the force of a freight train. A hard blow slammed into the back of his head.

And the world went black.

Melissa's ears were ringing. She couldn't hear much, but they were alive.

"Clay?" Her voice sounded muffled to her own ears. His weight was pressed against her back, pro-tecting her from the fallout. But he wasn't moving at all. "Clay?"

No. No, no.

Frantically, she tried wiggling out from under him, but he was heavy in his turnout clothes, a deadweight centered right on top of her.

"Help! Help us!"

What if—no, she wouldn't think that. He was okay. He had to be. She wasn't sure how long she struggled to free herself, but suddenly his body was lifted off her. Quickly she sat up to see some of his teammates, as well as hers, surrounding them. Clay's captain and Zack Knight were gently placing him onto his back.

She crawled to her lover, heart jammed in her throat. "Clay?"

"Let them work on him," Shane said, crouching beside her to lay a hand on her shoulder.

Her hand went over her mouth as tears spilled down her cheeks. Clay was too still, his face pale. Hurriedly they opened his turnout coat and loosened his clothing. Howard checked his pulse as the rest of them held their breaths.

"He's breathing," he said, and the relief was palpable. "But he's not out of the woods."

"He's got a head injury." Zack held up his hand, which was covered in blood.

Helplessly she watched as they got him hooked to an IV and monitored his vitals. He had to live. She was finally happy with a man she loved.

"He's survived much worse," Shane said gently. "Try not to worry."

"I'll try," she said with a sob. Shane's arm went around her, and she leaned into his comfort.

In minutes, they had him ready to transport. Julian said she could ride in the back with him and Clay. Zack would drive the ambulance. She didn't care who drove as long as she could be at his side.

Once they had Clay loaded into the back, she climbed in after him and Julian. The back doors were secured, and soon they were bouncing over the road headed back to town. Julian strapped an oxygen mask over Clay's face, but he hadn't stirred so far.

"Do you think he'll be okay?" she asked anxiously.

"Yeah, I do. He's come too far to go down like this." Julian's dark eyes grew suspiciously wet, and he shook his head. "Sorry. It's been a night."

"Yeah. How's Tonio?" She knew he was upset about his brother being shot, too. He had to be under tremendous strain, and yet he was holding up.

"He'll be fine. He was conscious and bitching when the guys from Station Two took him in." He paused. "I'm anxious to see him, though."

"I can imagine. I got to him as fast as I could, I want you to know that."

He glanced at her in surprise. "I never thought different. You did the best you could, and you got to him fast. Thank you."

"Don't thank me, thank his decision to wear his vest. It literally saved his life tonight."

They fell silent, and she watched Clay as his partner

took good care of him, cleaning the head wound and talking to him quietly. Once or twice she thought she saw a twitch behind his eyelids, but he didn't wake up.

At the hospital, Clay was whisked away to the exam room. Left with nothing to do but worry, she paced the waiting room, unable to take much comfort in the reassurances of their friends. She wouldn't rest until she knew Clay was going to be fine.

"Melissa? Honey?"

At the breathless voice, she turned to see Charlene hurrying into the emergency room. Immediately she drew Clay's mom into a hug. "Who called you?"

"The hospital," she said tearfully. "What's happened to my boy? I swear I can't take it if he's hurt as badly as before. I don't know if he has another fight like that left in him."

"There was an explosion and he was hit in the head by flying debris. We don't know anything yet, but he was breathing on his own when we got here."

"That's some good news, then."

"Yes. We'll have to wait and see what the doctor says."

"I wish I had a dollar for every time I've heard that over the last year."

"I know. I'm sorry."

The older woman patted her hand. "It's not your fault. My son has a dangerous job, and that's just something I have to live with. You, too, if you're going to stick around for the long haul."

"I plan to, if he'll have me."

"Oh, something tells me he will."

About thirty minutes later, an older doctor walked out of the double doors from the examination area. "Mrs. Montana?"

"Yes, that's me." Charlene pushed to her feet and clasped her trembling hands.

"Could I speak to you in private?"

"This is his girlfriend and these are his friends," she said, waving a hand impatiently. "Anything you say to me, you can say in front of them."

He nodded. "Your son has a moderate concussion, but there's no swelling on the brain and no permanent damage that we could detect." His words were met with a round of relieved exclamations. "In short, he's had the wind knocked out of him, has some bruising, and will have a hell of a headache for a couple of days, but he should be fine."

"How soon can he be released?" Charlene asked.

"Given his prior serious head injury, I want to keep him overnight for observation, but he should be able to go home tomorrow. We're moving him to a regular room for the night, then you can see him briefly. He'll need his rest."

Briefly my ass. Just let the doc try to drive them away and they'd see what happened.

In less than an hour, which seemed an eternity, they had him in a room. Melissa let Charlene visit him first, because she figured his mom would like some alone time with her son. The woman had been through so much worry for months, she deserved to see him first and be reassured.

About a half an hour later, she hugged Melissa and departed for home with the promise to see them both the next day. Then Melissa went into Clay's room, sat at his bedside, and took one of his hands.

His hand was warm and solid under hers, a reassurance that he was alive. That he'd wake up tomorrow. Hopefully sooner. Was it her imagination, or did his face seem to have more color? He definitely looked better. His chest rose and fell in a reassuring rhythm that made her tension ease.

He's going to be okay. And he's not going anywhere.

And she was going to take care of him when he was released tomorrow. She would have to find out whether he wanted to rest at his house or hers—but he would submit to being spoiled, at least for a day or two.

Clay was hers, and she wasn't ever letting go.

12

Consciousness returned slowly.

Clay emerged from the depths of a black hole and gradually became aware of his aching body. The quiet, terribly familiar sounds around him. *The hospital again. What happened? Right, the explosion . . . Jesus Christ.*

There were a couple of major differences in his stay this time—he could form a coherent thought, and he could move. He wiggled his fingers and toes to prove it. So, he wasn't out of commission this time. Thank God.

His head was splitting, though, like someone evil was driving a spike through the back of his neck. Repeatedly and with great sadistic pleasure.

I'm alive, though. I can deal with the rest.

"Clay?"

"M-Melissa?" His throat was dry as sandpaper.

"I'm here." A warm, soft hand gripped his. "Right here, sweetie. Open your eyes for me?"

It took several tries, but he managed. At first the form above him was blurry, but gradually his beautiful girl came into focus. Her relieved expression and broad smile made his heart leap as he squeezed her hand.

"Hey," he croaked.

"Welcome back to the land of the living. You have a pretty hard head, you know that?"

"Doesn't feel so hard right now. Kind of like mush."

Reaching out, she combed her fingers through his hair. He moaned in bliss.

"You're going to be fine. You got lucky. They're going to let you go home later today, as long as you're being watched."

"You can watch me all you want." He gave her a lopsided smile.

"That's my plan."

He thought about last night. "So, what happened at the compound after I was knocked out?"

"The fight was pretty much over," she said. "The rest of my uncle's men were hauled to jail, where they'll be charged with making illegal hooch, attempting to evade arrest, attempted murder of police officers, and a host of other things. It's done."

"Are you upset about your uncle's death? I mean, how he died . . ."

She shook her head, lips pressed into a firm line. "His death was gruesome, but fitting. He went out exactly the way he deserved, and I don't feel sorry for that."

"Good. I don't want you feeling any sort of guilt, because it wasn't your fault. He made his choices, and he reaped what he sowed."

"Exactly."

"How's my boy feeling?" Charlene stood in the doorway, smiling at the two of them.

"Hi, Mom."

She marched forward, a determined expression on her face. "Now, what the holy hell do you mean by getting thrown in here again? Are you *trying* to send me to an early grave?"

Clay bit back a sigh and resigned himself to being grilled about yesterday's events. She wouldn't rest until she had every detail about last night. He knew his mother well.

Fortunately, Melissa was there to fill in the blanks, and to take over when she noticed Clay's eyes drooping. Finally his mother said good-bye with a promise to see him when he was released and settled somewhere. It remained to be seen whether he'd stay at Melissa's house or his own.

One day soon, he hoped they were one and the same.

Several hours later, Clay was being wheeled out by a nurse, Melissa right beside him. Tiredness showed in her eyes, even when she smiled. She had to be exhausted from sitting with him all night, but she never once complained.

"Your place?" she asked as she pulled out of the parking lot.

"Yours. It's more relaxing there. We can stop by mine and get some of my clothes."

"Sounds good. You can sit on the back porch and watch the horses. It'll help you heal faster."

"Wrong. *You're* the one who'll help me heal faster. That and the prospect of getting you naked." He gave her a wink, and loved her throaty laugh.

"Sweet talker. You must be feeling better."

"Hey, there's nothing wrong with my little head."

"When it comes to a man, there rarely is."

"There's a reason the athletic cup was invented before the helmet, you know. We have our priorities straight."

"No, that's exactly why men have a shorter life expectancy than women."

"I think that's an arguable generalization."

"It's a fact."

"Let's say you're right. Would you rather have a smart man or a man who can pound you into the mattress all night?" he pointed out.

"Can't I have both?"

"You can if you have me." He smirked.

"You're impossible," she said, rolling her eyes.

"That's why you love me."

"One of the many reasons I love you."

"Damn, you know just what to say," he said softly. "I love you, too, beautiful."

She took his hand and they drove the rest of the way to his place in comfortable silence. Clay made short work of stuffing a few things into his duffel bag, and then they were on their way again. He was happy to head to her place. The idea of making his home outside the city limits appealed greatly, and he wondered if someday she'd consider letting him move in with her.

One step at a time.

Twenty minutes later, she pulled into her garage. Getting out of the car, he shouldered his duffel with a wince. The debris had hit his back as well, and he was sore, with a pretty spectacular bruise between his shoulder blades, or so he was told. He considered himself damned lucky he still had a brain inside his skull.

"I want you to rest," Melissa said as she let them inside the house.

"If I have to lounge in bed anymore, I'll go nuts."

"How about on the back porch in a comfy chair?"

He perked up. "With a beer in hand, sure."

"Um, no." She frowned. "Not so soon after a head injury. You should know that."

"Aww, give me a break. I haven't even had a pain pill today."

"And if you show signs of confusion, or have nausea or vomiting, you can bet the alcohol will make it worse."

"Damn," he said, deflating some. "You're right. Soda it is."

"Coming right up." She gave him a cheeky wink. "Put your stuff away and I'll meet you on the porch."

"Deal."

While she went to the kitchen, he walked down the hallway to her master bedroom and set the bag on the chair in the corner of her room. Then he went to the French doors leading out to the wide, spacious porch overlooking the back of the property, opened them, and headed outside.

He loved it out here. The peace and quiet, the serene view of the horses grazing lazily from spot to spot, were the best medicine in the world. Hearing footsteps on the boards, he turned to his lady. "I could sit out here forever and never move again."

"I know the feeling. My aunt loved it out here, too." She took a seat in the lounger beside his.

"You miss her."

"Every single day. She saved me. More than that, she loved me." She was silent for a few moments, looking out into the distance. "My uncle wanted to keep me from her, and from the only stability I'd known since my parents died. I never understood why. He hated me, and it showed in everything he said and did, every single day. Why keep me around?"

"Because he could. He seemed like the kind of asshole who'd enjoy the power trip, even over a helpless little girl."

"You nailed that one." She shivered. "Is it wrong of me to be glad he's dead?"

"No. He was a mean bastard and made your life hell. He also made his choices, and they led him to his fate." Clay took her hand. "I'm just sorry you had to witness it."

"I don't think I'll ever get that horrid scene out of my head."

Neither did he, but he didn't want either of them to dwell on it. "How're your guys? Everyone okay? Shit, how's Tonio?"

"He's doing pretty well, considering. Bitching up a storm about wanting to go home, which is much better than the alternative. Thank God he was wearing his vest."

"Yeah." The man would be dead right now if he hadn't been. "I know Julian has to be losing his mind."

"He was, but he's calmed down a lot," she said. "Seeing that his brother is going to be fine has helped."

"When will the doctors let him out?"

"In a couple of days, barring infection or some other complication."

"That's great news." He couldn't fathom how Julian would've recovered had he lost his brother. Last year, Tonio had barely survived a beating by a gang led by his girlfriend's brother. The man must have nine lives.

"Hey," she said, tugging on his hand with a soft smile. "No need to look so broody. Everyone is fine. Our side ten, bad guys zero. Game over."

"Sure." He smiled at her. But was it? An unsettled feeling churned in his gut, and he wasn't sure why. It all seemed too neat and tidy, and it was hard to believe her uncle's vendetta had come to an end.

But he's dead. We saw him burn. His men are either pushing up daisies, too, or in jail.

"That's still too serious a face, handsome."

Suddenly he found himself with a lapful of warm, soft woman. Gentle hands cupped his face and drew him in for a slow, passionate kiss. His swift reaction proved that not every part of him was bruised and sore.

The kiss went on for several moments, their tongues tangling together as he breathed in her sweet scent. His fingers buried themselves in her hair and he relished the slide of the silky tresses through them. When she finally pulled back, they were both panting. He was hard as a rock and there was no way she could've missed it, sitting on his lap like she was.

"Let's retreat to your room," he murmured.

"Your head—"

"Aches horribly, I assure you." He ground his crotch into her for emphasis.

"You're incorrigible."

"You wouldn't want me any other way."

"You're right."

He stood, and she clung to him with her legs around his waist and arms around his neck as he headed back into her bedroom. Once there, he laid her carefully on the bed and pulled off his shirt. Next went his shoes, jeans, and underwear as she watched hungrily.

"I'll never get tired of seeing you get naked," she told him.

"You might when I'm old and fat."

"You'll never be either of those things to me."

"You're so damned good for my ego. But you're the gorgeous one." Crawling onto the bed, he started working on her jeans.

Unzipping them, he slid them down her hips, revealing the lacy red panties underneath. He adored this woman and her love of feminine things, which seemed so at odds with her no-nonsense, sometimes brash, cop personality. She could hold her own against any man.

But she was *all* woman.

All mine.

Clay couldn't wait to plunge deep inside her, but he didn't want to rush this. He slid her panties down her legs. Then with his fingers, he parted her folds and began to stroke, getting her ready for him. In moments she was slick and wet, writhing against his touch. He loved how responsive she was, never shy about expressing her desires. Unable to draw things out, he positioned himself at her entrance and pressed inside.

"Sorry, baby," he breathed. "This isn't going to last long."

"Just move, please." Her breath came in short gasps, her green eyes heavy-lidded.

He began to slide in and out of her wet heat, relishing how she hugged his cock. Wrapping her arms around him, she clung to his shoulders as he picked up the tempo, soon pounding into her with abandon. From her hoarse cries, she didn't mind the fast and furious fucking at all. This was a celebration. They were alive, and together.

Too soon, Clay felt himself quicken, and he didn't want it to end. However, he was powerless to hold back the orgasm that barreled through him like a nuclear blast. He felt her follow, clenching around him. Stiffening, he pumped his seed deep inside her welcoming body, on and on until they were sated.

After a few moments, he shifted to the side and pulled her with him, snuggling her back against his chest. He kissed her hair and inhaled her scent, beyond grateful they'd made it through the confrontation with her uncle.

"How are you feeling?" she murmured.

"I'm fine." His head throbbed and he was sore, but he'd live. "Let's nap, baby."

Pressing closer, she muttered something unintelligible and he let the warm peace envelop him, and carry him away.

Clay wasn't sure what had awakened him.

The room was dark now, and a glance at the clock told him they'd slept past dinner. It was almost eleven. They must've been more tired than he'd thought.

Suddenly he became aware that light was flickering through the window. Strangely, it was dancing in a yellow-orange glow. "What the hell?"

Rolling out of bed, he padded to the window—and gaped at the sight, stunned. "Shit!"

Spurred into action, he turned from the window and rushed to the lamp by the bed, flipping it on. Then he yanked on his jeans, calling to the still-sleeping form huddled in the bed.

"Melissa! Wake up!"

His shout immediately had her sitting up, blinking toward him in confusion. "What? What's going on?" Her gaze cleared as she took in his panic.

"The barn's on fire! Call for help!"

"Oh my God," she moaned, face paling, eyes wide. Quickly, she slid out of bed and reached for the cell phone he tossed at her.

"I'm going down there to get the horses out and see if I can stop the blaze."

"Be careful!"

He gave her a quick kiss, then turned and ran for the door, shirtless and wearing only his jeans and boots. In the background, he could hear her talking to a dispatcher, and prayed that whichever station got the call, they would hurry. It had been a rough couple of days for the Sugarland Fire Department— and it was about to get worse.

Bounding down the stairs, he hit the bottom and kept running without even stopping. Through the living room, toward the back of the house, through the kitchen and out the back door. As he dashed down the steps of the porch, he saw flames licking up one side of the barn, heard the panicked whinnies of the horses desperately wanting to be free.

Heart in his throat, he bypassed going for the water hose—the modest stream of water it would provide wasn't going to help now—and went straight for the barn. It was the height of stupidity to run into a burning structure without the proper gear, but he wasn't going to let the animals die. Not if he could help them.

Shoving the big rolling door aside, he peered into the thickening smoke. He could just make out the shapes of the three horses whirling frantically about in their stalls. One of them was kicking at the stall door, but he couldn't tell which one.

Clay darted inside and ran directly to the nearest stall, working quickly at the latch. The flames were spreading and the terrorized animals were going to hurt themselves trying to get out if he didn't hurry. And he was going to be in trouble too, very soon. The heat and smoke were stinging his eyes, clogging his lungs.

The latch gave and Clay swung the gate open, moving out of the way as the horse bolted from the stall, out of the barn to safety. He'd managed to save one, but relief was short-lived. Two more to go.

Next up was the big bay gelding. By the time he made it to the stall, he was coughing up a lung. Quitting wasn't an option, though, and he worked fast on that latch, too. Thank God that one opened easily, and the bay was soon galloping to freedom. One more to go.

As Clay turned, he caught a glimpse of a figure moving toward him through the smoke. At first he thought it was Melissa, and he yelled out in fear. "What the hell are you doing in here?"

But it wasn't his lover who appeared in front of him. The figure of a man approached through the murk, and Clay was relieved that help had arrived. The sneer on the man's face and the long board clutched in his hand quickly disabused him of that notion.

Clay barely had time to avoid the makeshift weapon swinging at his head. He ducked and it sailed past his ear, crashing into the wall behind him. "Hey! What the fu—"

The board swung again, this time catching him hard in the right thigh and sending a shockwave of pain clear to the bone. With a shout, he threw himself into his attacker, sending them both to the hard-packed ground. They rolled in the dirt, the other man doing his best to get Clay pinned. *Not gonna happen.*

"Who the fuck . . . are you?" he panted, grappling with the big bastard. Looking up, past the man's head, he saw the roof was on fire. "Shit! We're both going to die, you stupid asshole!"

"You're the one who's gonna die," the man growled, trying to get his hands around Clay's throat. "For getting me sent back to prison!"

"What?" For a few seconds, he couldn't compute his attacker's meaning.

And when it dawned on him, his blood ran cold.

"You're Foster Ryan," he said, coughing. He could barely make out the man's form, but what he could see of his face was enough. Foster was so like his father—filled with hatred. "You're the one who hit my ambulance and robbed me of a year of my life, you son of a bitch!"

"If you hadn't pulled into that intersection, I wouldn't have been caught with my stash and sent back to the joint."

"Typical scum," Clay snarled. "Your fuckups are always someone else's fault."

"I'm gonna kill you, and then I'm going to make my traitorous cousin pay. Or maybe I'll torture her first while you watch, make her scream before I kill her, then I'll take care of you after."

The horror of that threat gave Clay the strength he needed to break the man's hold. Surging up, he shoved at Foster hard, throwing him off and rolling out from under him. Staggering to his feet, he lurched for the last stall door and slammed his hand into the stubborn latch twice, finally managing to slide it open. He barely jumped out of the way as the last frantic horse burst from the stall and galloped out of the barn.

That accomplished, he started for the wide door, legs like rubber. Just short of his goal, he was tackled from behind. Twisting his body, he punched his attacker in the side of the head—once, twice—and stunned the bastard enough to free himself once more. Scrambling forward, he made it outside, fell to his knees, and heaved the fresh air in gulps.

"Clay? Oh my God, are you all right?"

Melissa. She dashed out the back door, the firelight illuminating her in its glow. Barefoot, dressed in jeans and a T-shirt, she was intent on getting to him.

Panic had him surging back to his feet. "Run," he croaked. "Get back in—"

"Foster?" Her eyes widened as she skidded to a stop a few feet away, staring at a spot behind him.

Clay whirled to see the man had followed him out

into the open and was gazing at Melissa with undisguised venom. In return, fury masked her face.

"You bastard! What have you done?" she yelled, hands balling into fists.

"I'm settling a score," he called back, smirking. "You didn't believe Dad was working alone, did you? Ooh, he didn't tell you."

"How did you escape from prison? When?" Anger warred with disbelief in her voice.

"Been out long enough to do some of Dad's dirty work. Who do you think took the shot at you? Didn't you recognize my voice that night?"

"You were the one in the cowboy hat," she whispered.

"Bingo! And who do you think *actually* ran you and that other pig off the road?" His laugh was low, dark, and angry. "You and your boyfriend need to pay, and I won't miss again."

With that, Foster reached around to the small of his back. Clay was moving, sprinting across the few feet between him and the other man before Foster swung his arm around, gun in his outstretched hand—pointing it at Melissa.

No!

Clay slammed his body into Foster's just as the weapon discharged with a deafening bang, making his ears ring. Driving the other man to the ground, he took stock of himself. *I'm not hit.*

But what about Melissa? Please, no.

Foster attempted to bring the gun up and point the muzzle at Clay, but Clay levered himself over the other man to pin him, grabbed his wrist, and beat his hand on the ground repeatedly, trying to dislodge the weapon. Panting with exertion, he risked a glance toward Melissa and was relieved to see her disappear inside the house again.

Please, call for backup. And stay inside, baby.

He knew his lady cop better than that, though. In the time he'd known her, she'd never backed down from a fight and he doubted she'd change that now.

"Let go of that gun, you fucker," Clay wheezed, slapping Foster's hand to the ground again.

"Eat shit," the man snarled. And promptly hurled a fistful of dirt into Clay's eyes.

Cursing, he shook his head and tried to wipe his face on his sleeve, but the dirt stung his already smoke-irritated eyes. It was just the opening his attacker needed.

The blow caught him on the side of the head, sending him toppling sideways. Foster immediately took advantage, punching him hard again, in the temple. Stunned, Clay fell onto his back, grasping blindly at the other man, to no avail.

He heard the sound of scuffling boots and looked up in time to see Foster scrambling to his feet, levering his arm downward. And Clay found himself staring straight up the muzzle of the man's gun.

"Good-bye, Montana."

Oh, God. To survive all he had and then die like this? What would happen to Melissa? His blood went cold as he anticipated the gunshot.

"Foster!"

Melissa's shout caught the other man's attention, and he turned to face her, eyes wide. Heart in his throat, Clay snapped his gaze to his lover. She was standing a few feet away with her legs braced apart, her own gun pointed at her cousin.

"Drop the weapon!" she yelled.

A split second of indecision flashed across his features before he returned his attention to Clay. The hatred blazing in the bastard's eyes told Clay the man wasn't going to be swayed from his decision. He thrust the gun toward Clay's face, finger tightening on the trigger.

Clay's heartbeat stuttered in his chest.

A gunshot split the air—and crimson spread across Foster's chest as his eyes widened in surprise. The man crumpled to the ground with a sickening thud, and Clay stared, gorge rising in his throat as Foster breathed his last.

"Clay! Are you all right?"

At Melissa's frantic voice, he pushed himself up to a sitting position, wincing in pain. His head and leg throbbed where Foster had struck him, but all told, things could have turned out much worse.

It could've been *his* brains splattered all over the ground instead.

"I'm okay," he said. Then Melissa dropped to her knees beside him, the gun falling from her hand, and he found himself with an armful of soft woman. Burying his face in her hair, he groaned and held her tight. "Thanks to you, I'm better than okay."

Sirens sounded in the distance, drawing closer. About fucking time.

"I wasn't going to stand there and watch him shoot you," she said fiercely. "He deserved what he got for trying to destroy what's mine. For trying to take you from me."

"My tough cop." Drawing back some, he caressed her face. "You're not going to get in trouble for this, are you? It was justifiable, right?"

Her expression softened, and she kissed him gently. "Everything will be fine. I'll have to complete a lot of damned paperwork and I'll probably be put on leave for a few days as a formality, but in the end I won't be penalized."

"Good to know." After glancing at Foster's body again, he looked back at her and swallowed hard. "He came here with the intention of luring us out with the fire. He was going to knock me out in the barn, leave me to burn, and then come after you. Makes me sick to think of how close he came to getting his wish."

"But he didn't. We'll be fine now, honey."

Red and blue flashing lights drew closer, the familiar noise of the fire truck's horn blasting through the night, heard above the raging fire behind them. The barn would be a total loss, but the structure could be replaced.

The quint pulled into the yard and Clay was gratified to see his own team in charge of the scene. Right behind them were two police cars moving fast up the drive. He'd never beheld a more welcome sight than the cavalry coming to the rescue—even if his lover had already dispatched their would-be murderer.

"Clay!" Six-Pack called, jogging toward them as the rest of the team started rolling out the hoses to battle the blaze. The captain stopped dead in his tracks, looking sick at the sight of Foster lying dead on the ground. "Jesus. Who the fuck is that?"

Clay pushed to his feet, helping Melissa up as well. "Cap, meet the late Foster Ryan. The man who cost me a year of my life in recovery after he hit our ambulance, and the asshole who broke out of prison and came back to settle a score."

The captain whistled softly and gave them both a sympathetic look. "Damn. I'm glad as hell he failed, but I'm sorry it had to come to this."

"Me, too," Melissa whispered.

Clay felt her tremble and tucked her into his side. He knew what was happening. The shock was hitting her hard now that the incident was over, and she was going to crash. Unfortunately, they had to wade through giving her colleagues in the PD a report, seeing her through the suspension of duties, and making sure the barn fire was out. Being able to rest was hours away.

Clay swayed a little on his feet and coughed violently. Melissa grabbed him around the waist and Six-Pack shook his head, eyeing him with a frown.

"Did you go into that burning barn?"

"Yeah." He coughed again. "Had to get the horses out, then Foster ambushed me. Clobbered me with a damned two-by-four."

The big man sighed. "Come on, let's get you checked out. And this had better be the absolute last time *either* of you get hurt, you hear me? Enough of that shit."

"Now that Foster and his father won't be crossing our paths anymore, the odds of us staying healthy are much better."

It's over. We're going to be okay.

Sure, it was going to be a long night. But they would get through it like they had every other challenge since she'd come into his life—together.

13

Peace and quiet. Coffee. And the man of my dreams. This is the life.

Melissa reclined in a chair on the back porch, jean-clad legs crossed at the ankles, bare feet propped on the railing, and sipped a cup of her favorite French roast. The horses were grazing, moving lazily along in the pasture beyond the fence, none the worse for wear after their ordeal. The vet had come by early the morning after the fire, and checked them over, pronouncing them healthy.

The one blight on the scenery was the burned husk of the barn, which stood as a stark reminder of all she and Clay could have lost. Against her will, her gaze drifted once again toward the blackened structure, and she shuddered. The love of her life had nearly died that night. The nightmarish sight of her vengeful cousin standing over Clay, a gun pointed at his head and ready to pull the trigger . . .

That memory was etched into her brain and would take a long time to fade—if it ever did.

The squeak of the back door sounded, followed by a familiar tread on the boards. Clay was striding toward her wearing nothing but a pair of sleep pants and a smile, his sandy blond hair tousled from bed. *God, I'm such a lucky bitch.*

He held a steaming mug of coffee in one hand as he took the chair beside her. The look he gave her was full of heat. "I woke up in bed this morning without a gorgeous redhead in my arms. Now why is that?"

Her body warmed. The man could get her worked up faster than anyone she'd known. "You looked so peaceful, I didn't want to wake you. You definitely needed the rest."

"So did you. This week has been a much-needed reprieve from the madness James and Foster perpetuated."

"What Foster did to you sickens me," she whispered, reaching over to take his hand. "You lost an entire year of your life because of the wreck he caused, and then he and my uncle had the gall to blame the fallout on you."

"They tried to kill us both. They wanted you dead

just because you were a cop." He looked away briefly, directing his glare out, over the pasture.

"Not just any cop, but because I was family and *betrayed* them by becoming one. I'm ashamed I was ever related to them."

Clay shook his head, his gaze softening as he smiled at her. "They were never your family in the way that mattered. You had your aunt to love and care for you, and now you have me. Not to mention all of our friends."

Happiness welled up inside her, and tears stung her eyes. "You're right. Damn, when did I turn into such a crybaby?"

"Since you learned you don't have to be the strong one all the time, and it's okay to lean on someone else—me."

Then he leaned over and brushed his lips against hers. What started as a sweet kiss turned sensual, fast. From day one, her lover had been a smoldering ember ready to explode into flames. She wouldn't have him any other way.

Just as the kiss deepened, promising to become more, the whine of engines sounded in the distance, coming up the driveway.

Groaning, she pulled back ruefully. "Visitors? Now? They have crappy timing."

He grinned sheepishly. "Yeah, I forgot to tell you Six-Pack called this morning, which is what woke me up. He wanted to make sure we were going to be home."

"Did he say why?"

"Nope. Just said to stay put and clear our day of whatever we had planned."

"Huh." Brows furrowed, she watched as the big pickup truck roared into view. The intriguing thing was the convoy of vehicles following behind it. All shapes, sizes, and models.

"What the hell?" Clay murmured, standing.

In the lead truck, she saw the big captain behind the wheel, and his wife, Kat, next to him. She peered at the vehicles behind the Paxtons' and her mouth fell open. "Your whole crew from the fire station must've shown up!"

"And a few more besides," Clay agreed, setting his coffee on a nearby table. "Let's go see what's up." He started forward but she tugged on his arm.

"Um, you're half-naked, Mr. Sexy."

"Oh." Looking down at himself, he flushed slightly. "Entertain the troops while I go throw on some clothes."

"Sure thing." She winked at him, earning a chuckle. Once he'd gone inside, she set her own mug down and jogged down the porch steps to join their visitors. Of which there were many.

Gaping in astonishment, she noted that not only were his friends among the arrivals, but several of her closest friends and colleagues from the police station as well. She blinked at the rig Shane was driving—a big flatbed trailer with a bulldozer loaded onto it. Other trucks were filled with all sorts of tools and materials. In particular, she noted a second flat-bed roll into view driven by Chris, and this one was loaded with two-by-fours.

One by one, the vehicles parked in every available space in her yard, front and back, the ones with the tools and heavy equipment rolling around back near the barn. As their friends parked, their wives and significant others emerged carrying grocery bags, coolers, pies, and an extra coffeemaker.

In that moment, she began to form an idea of what was going on, and her throat grew tight. Her eyes filled with tears all over again.

"Surprise!" Kat called out. She hurried forward, carrying what looked like a pound cake wrapped with plastic. "Nothing like having a whole boatload of people descend on your peace and quiet first thing in the morning!"

"You guys," Melissa said hoarsely as her friends came forward. "Is this what I think it is?"

"What's going on?" Clay called, jogging down the steps to meet them. Smiling, he came to stand beside Melissa and draped an arm around her waist. He'd dressed quickly in a pair of worn jeans and a T-shirt.

Six-Pack was grinning. "Sorry about the lack of notice, but this was meant to be a surprise. Who's ready for an old-fashioned barn raising?"

Melissa's hand went over her mouth and she choked on a sob. "Really?"

"Really," the big captain confirmed, eyes warm. "What are friends for?"

"I don't know what to say." The thought and planning that had gone into this, the caring, overwhelmed her. "I can't believe I thought for one minute that I didn't have any family left."

Six-Pack smiled and said gently, "No one knows better than me that family is made up of the people who love you. And we're here to show you that you'll never be without family as long as we're around. Right?" he called out loud.

The crowd sent up a cheer of agreement, and the tears slipped freely down Melissa's cheeks. After everything was said and done, she'd been right to return to Sugarland. To face her past and make this place, these fine people, her own.

And to claim the man she loved.

"You're so right," she said. "I can't thank you all enough for this. You don't know what it means."

"Yeah, we do," Shane replied, beaming at her. "We've all needed help, and now it's our turn to give back." He turned to Drew and Blake. "Boys, help us get this stuff unloaded so we can get started."

"Yes, sir!" Drew called, running off with Blake on his heels.

A few of the crowd laughed, and Melissa watched the young man fondly, glad beyond words that Drew had survived the shooting. So many lives would've been destroyed that day had the outcome been different.

Kat came forward, linking her free arm with Melissa's. "Come on, let's get this food in the kitchen. Everyone's going to be hungry, sooner rather than later once they start working."

A few of the other women followed them inside and helped get the food, drinks, paper plates, cups, and coolers situated for easy pickings. Melissa enjoyed talking and laughing with them, and realized she was bonding with other women for the first time. For a woman who worked in a male-dominated environment, it was wonderful to let her hair down and be one of the girls.

"Damn, that's some fine man-flesh out there," Cara said with a sigh, peering out the kitchen window at the activity. "Are we lucky, gals, or what?"

There was a round of enthusiastic agreement. That was followed by a suggestion to make mimosas, which was met by even more enthusiasm. Out came the champagne and orange juice, and much laughter, not to mention gossip about their men, ensued.

Outside, the bulldozer roared to life, and Shane proceeded to clear off the rubble of the old barn, amid much "help" from Taylor—mostly his best friend yelling out directions, telling Shane what he ought to do and how. Shane flipped his friend the bird and pretty much ignored him. Melissa and the other women giggled as they watched, sipping their drinks on the porch.

Shirts were stripped off as the day grew hot, and the men hammered. The women certainly didn't complain about the view. Slowly, the framework began to take shape—a bigger and better barn than before. Big enough to expand her stock if she wanted.

Out of the ashes, something new and good was being built. Something that had nothing to do with the barn itself. Something solid, and lasting.

Friendships. And family. The only ones who really mattered.

It was the best day Melissa could remember in a very, very long time.

The barn raising had actually taken two days. The framework and walls had gone up the first day, and that was the hardest part. On the second day, they finished out the stalls and detail work inside.

Now it was done, their friends gone home, and Clay was sprawled in the recliner in the living room, cataloging his aches. They were the good kind, brought about by hours of honest hard labor. He smiled to himself, thinking how grateful he was to be alive and well, to feel *normal*. This time last year, he'd been fighting for his life.

These days, he was looking forward to his future.

Footsteps came from the kitchen, and he glanced up as Melissa padded into the room. She'd made so many trips to gaze out the kitchen windows at the new barn, he was surprised she hadn't worn a path in the floorboards.

"I can't get over how great it looks," she said, not for the first time.

"Wait until we get it painted, it'll look even better." He smiled, holding out a hand to beckon her to sit in his lap. She quickly obliged, settling her bottom on his thighs and nestling in with her face in the curve of his neck.

"I don't even care about paint. I'm just thankful we have such great friends."

"We do, don't we? I don't know how I would've survived the past year without them."

Pulling back, she cupped his face. "I'm sorrier than you'll ever know that my cousin was responsible for what happened to you."

"Stop," he ordered. "None of that was your fault, and it's time for both of us to move past it. Let's concentrate on where we go from here."

Letting out a deep breath, she gave him a playful smile, relaxing in his arms. "And where might that be?"

His brows rose. "Oh, I can think of a good place. Like you and me, and a nice, hot shower to get rid of all this dirt and sweat."

"I think I like you best when you're dirty." She leered at him to emphasize the double entendre.

Urging her to stand, he pushed out of the chair

and scooped her into his arms, chuckling at her squeak of delight. "I like me best when I'm dirty, too. Why don't we go see if we can find out just how filthy I can be?"

"I like the way you think, even if I already have a good idea."

Clay relished the feel of his woman in his arms, and loved carrying her up the stairs. Something he couldn't have done just a few months ago. He didn't take such a simple thing for granted anymore. Every moment was a miracle to him.

Upstairs, he set her down and took her hand, leading her into the bathroom. They stripped quickly, and she reached for the faucet on the large bathtub, turning on the water and then plugging the drain.

"Thought we were going for a shower?" he asked.

"Wrong. We're taking a bubble bath!"

He groaned dramatically. "Now I really have to turn in my man card. If it smells like flowers, I'm not getting in."

Stark naked, she held up the bottle and turned to face him, wiggling her hips. "You sure about that?"

"Shit." Heat surged into his groin, and his cock began to rise. "Never mind. Who cares what it smells like?"

She giggled. "I thought so. It's vanilla, by the way."

"Well, that's not so bad. Smelling like a bowl of ice cream sounds better than reeking like a floral shop any day."

"Mmm, ice cream." She eyed him hungrily, pouring a generous amount of soap into the stream. "The better to eat you up."

He couldn't get into the water fast enough. Settling into the steamy heat with a sigh of pleasure, he held his hand out to her. Taking it, she climbed in, and he turned her around so that she was sitting with her back to his front. Then he spread his legs and pulled her close, nestling her bottom against his cock and balls, the former riding the crack of her ass.

"Someone likes bubble baths after all," she teased.

"Little Clay likes *you* in the bubble bath with *me*."

"Not so little," she murmured.

"Glad you think so. I'm kinda stuck with him."

"Mmm," she purred, reaching behind her to wrap a hand around his neck. "I can't think of a single thing that makes me happier."

"How about this?"

Pressing kisses into her hair, he scooped up a mound of bubbles and spread them onto one pert nipple. He loved the little noises of appreciation she made as he plucked the tip, giving it plenty of attention. She arched into his touch like a kitten wanting to be petted, and he gave her what she asked for.

The other nub received equal attention and she moaned, begging for more. Obliging, he slid his palm down her belly to the juncture of her thighs and rubbed the folds of her sex. Spreading her legs, she raised her hips and turned her head to meet him in a kiss. A deep, hungry one that stoked the fire inside him had him hard as a steel rod in seconds.

Breaking the kiss, he panted, "Lift up, baby. Brace your hands on the side of the tub."

Carefully, she rose to her knees and bent over, widening her stance for him. She looked like a gorgeous, redheaded sea goddess sent to tempt him beyond endurance. He almost wished they were making love someplace tropical, on a beach with waves lapping at their toes.

But he certainly wasn't complaining.

"You're so beautiful," he whispered. His fingers parted her, then delved inside, gently stroking to make sure she was ready.

"Please."

She didn't have to ask twice. Maneuvering onto his knees, he got into position behind her and brought the head of his cock to her entrance. Slowly, he pressed inside her welcoming heat and groaned. He couldn't come. Not yet.

Her channel around him fit like a glove, squeezing him deliciously, making him crazy. This wasn't going to last long, but he didn't care. They'd do it again and again.

They had forever.

Soon he was moving in and out of her, and the wonderful friction sent jolts of pleasure along every nerve ending. His tempo increased until he was pumping with abandon, gripping her hips, vaguely aware of water sloshing all over the tiled floor. He couldn't care less about that.

"Yes," she breathed. "Fuck me hard!'

That plea, the assault on his senses, sent his desire spiraling out of control. It was more than he could take, and too soon his release boiled over. Unstoppable. He gave a shout as he shuddered and held still, buried deep inside her. With a cry, she climaxed, her walls spasming around his cock, milking him dry.

"What you do to me," he said, lost in the glow.

"Same thing you do to me—you rock my world, every time." He heard the smile in her voice.

Gently pulling free, he helped her sit again and then grabbed the soap. Washing together was fun, and more water found the floor. Neither of them cared.

After they were clean, he helped her dry off and then led her to the bedroom. Together, they sprawled on the bed and she snuggled into him, resting her head on his chest. For the longest time, he simply held her close, enjoying her warm body wrapped around him, her heartbeat, the sound of her breathing. He stroked her hair, liking how she played idly with his chest.

"I love you," she said quietly. "I never knew it was possible to love anyone this way. I never thought love was for me."

"I love you, too." He squeezed her tight. "I'd hoped love was for me, someday. This time last year, I believed I'd never have the chance to find out because

I was too broken. Just goes to show how life can turn on a dime, and not just for the worst. It can change for the better, when you least expect it."

Resting her chin on his chest, she gazed at him with such love, it took his breath away.

"Yes, it sure can," she said. "I have everything now I've ever wanted—a man I love, who loves me. Family, friends. My life was completed the day I met you."

"Mine, too, baby. Mine, too."

He was a damned lucky man.

And he'd never, ever forget that as long as he lived.

About the Author

Jo Davis is the author of the popular Firefighters of Station Five series (*Ride the Fire, Line of Fire*), the Sugarland Blue series (*On the Run, In His Sights*), and, as J. D. Tyler, the Alpha Pack paranormal romance series (*Chase the Darkness, Wolf's Fall*). A multiple finalist in the Colorado Romance Writers Award of Excellence and a finalist for the Bookseller's Best Award, she has captured the HOLT Medallion Award of Merit and has been a two-time nominee for the Australian Romance Readers Award.

Visit her at jodavis.net, facebook.com/Jo-Davis-1095 47185743800, and twitter.com/JoDavisAuthor.

Connect with Berkley Publishing Online!

For sneak peeks into the newest releases, news on all your favorite authors, book giveaways, and a central place to connect with fellow fans—

"Like" and follow Berkley Publishing!

facebook.com/BerkleyPub
twitter.com/BerkleyPub
instagram.com/BerkleyPub

1844